Black Fox Literary

M A G A Z I N E

Black Fox Literary Magazine is a print and online literary magazine published biannually.

Copyright © 2022 by *Black Fox Literary Magazine.*

All Rights Reserved.

Issue 22 Cover Art: *Jellyfish* by Hannah Vitiello

ISBN: 978-1-7336240-8-4

Editor's Note

It is with great joy that we present to you Issue 22 of *Black Fox Literary Magazine*. One thing is for certain regarding this pandemic: writers are writing! We were humbled by a record number of outstanding submissions and faced some tough decisions. After much consideration, we are thrilled to present to our readers the very best *Black Fox* selections.

Please come find us on social media @Blackfoxlit and share your favorite pieces from Issue 22. We'd love to see photos of you perusing the pages in ordinary and outlandish places alike!
As always, we thank all of our contributors, present and past. We are honored to feature your work in our pages.

We are truly yours,

~ The Editors
Racquel and Elizabeth

Meet the BFLM Staff

Editor:

Racquel Henry is a Trinidadian writer, editor, and writing coach with an MFA from Fairleigh Dickinson University. She is also the Editor-in-Chief at Voyage YA Journal and owns the writing studio, Writer's Atelier, in Maitland, FL. Racquel has been a featured author, presenter, and moderator at writing conferences and MFA residencies across the US. She is the author of the novelette, Holiday on Park, Letter to Santa, and The Writer's Atelier Little Book of Writing Affirmations. Her fiction, poetry, and nonfiction have appeared in various literary magazines and anthologies. When she's not working, you can find her watching Hallmark Christmas movies.

Managing Editor:

Elizabeth Sheets is a writer and an editorial assistant for the Journal of Proteome Research. She earned a MA in Narrative Studies from Arizona State University. As a student, Elizabeth developed a passion for prison education. She has taught writing classes inside local prisons and corresponds with inmate writers about their creative work. Elizabeth enjoys a wide variety of different reading material. Some of her favorite authors are Elizabeth Gilbert, John Jakes, Roxane Gay, Stephen King, Anne Rice, Brandon Mull, Aimee Bender, and J.K. Rowling. Elizabeth's fiction, nonfiction, and poetry appear in Kalliope – A Consortium of New Voices, Black Fox Literary Magazine, Mulberry Fork Review, and Apeiron Review.

Social Media Manager:

Megan Fuentes is an author and the administrative assistant for Writer's Atelier. Her favorite things in the world include iced coffee, office supplies, and telling you about those things. And writing, too. And lists! She is @fuentespens online, and her website is https://fuentespens.ink.

Contents:

Cover Art

Jellyfish by Hannah Vitiello

One Horn
By Stephen Page

The crepuscular sky above a range of mountains lightened to a deep blue, then to a soft blue, then to white, then orange, then a blood-red spot dripped up out of the ridgeline. A few miles away, near a beach, a seagull rode an air current above a long wave row curling in upon the shore. The seagull cawed then dove into the water behind the wave and rose with a large piece of flotsam in its beak. Thirty or forty other gulls quickly gathered in the area, screeching and cawing and diving.

Farther down the beach, where the wind complained and the waves crashed roaringly upon the sand, two young men were laughing. They were wearing dark gray shirts, black jeans, black shoes, and thick leather belts with 9-millimeter pistols holstered on the right side and black riot batons slung on the left. Sewn onto the left sleeves of their shirts were crimson and gold security crests. They had neatly trimmed hair. Parked in the sand behind them was a pickup truck with security crests upon both open doors.

Jonathan and Mike were laughing and attempting, quite unsuccessfully, to skip flat beach stones over the large waves. Jonathan pointed behind them to the top of the mountain range. The mountains had bled a sanguine sun. It flipped suddenly to yellow a degree or two above the ridgeline.

Jonathan, smiling, threw down the remaining stones in his hands.

"I guess we should get going," he said, dusting the sand off his hands.

"In a hurry to get on the road?" asked Mike.

"Naw, it's just… we haven't checked the last complex is all."

Mike glanced back at the sea, dropped his stones and pointed. "Look," he said.

Four dolphins glided parallel to the beach, behind the curling waves, and as they moved, their bodies rose and submerged gracefully, like effortless, spiritual weavers of the waters.

Jonathan and Mike watched the dolphins until they had well passed, then Jonathan looked at his watch.

"We only have an hour left," he said. "Gives us just enough time to check the last place and get back to the station for check out time."

Mike, still looking in the direction of the disappearing dolphins, said, "Yeah."

They turned and walked toward the truck.

"I saw your bike packed up last night when we started work," said Mike.

"Yeah," Jonathan said.

"Hey!" said Mike. "You can learn to speak with a Brooklyn accent, like Brando." He hit Jonathan in the shoulder. They laughed.

Mike climbed in the driver side and closed the door. Jonathan hesitated. Some fifty feet behind the truck was a young man sitting upon a seawall. He had long blonde hair, was wearing a red T-shirt, blue jeans, work boots, and was smoking a cigarette and drinking a beer in a can.

"Let's go," said Mike.

"Hey," Jonathan said, looking at Mike. "Doesn't that dude over there look out of place?"

Mike looked in the rear-view mirror.

"Where," said he.

Jonathan looked at the empty place where the young man had been.

"C'mon," said Mike.

Jonathan got in and stared at the dashboard.

The truck rolled down Main Street. There were two clothing shops, a surfboard shop, one restaurant, a café, a bar, a hotel, and a post office. All, save the restaurant and the hotel were not yet open.

Two teenage boys in black wet suits, carrying surfboards and heading toward the beach, crossed in front of truck.

There was no other movement on the street.

"This is a boring town," Jonathan said. "Nothing, I mean absolutely nothing ever happens here. Can't say I'll miss it much."

"Well, I heard New York's a little more exciting," said Mike.

As they passed the open restaurant, a gray-haired man exited the front doors. He was wearing a red plaid hunting cap, which he had pulled low over his eyes, a red plaid shirt, khakis, and brown boots. He stopped outside the doors of the restaurant and lit a thin cigar. Jonathan looked at him.

The truck continued to head toward the end of town. The old man, with his eyes shadowed, puffed on the thin cigar. He walked to edge of street. He pulled his hat even lower over his eyes and continued to watch the truck while puffing on his cigar. Jonathan leaned forward and looked in the side mirror. There was no one where the man once was. Jonathan rubbed his eyes.

At the first corner, two girls, both nineteen, wrapped in brightly colored wet suits and carrying surfboards, neared the crosswalk. They smiled, showing large white teeth, and waved at Jonathan and Mike. Jonathan and Mike waved back.

"Something's I guess I'll miss," Jonathan said.

"They'll be plenty of that in New York," said Mike.

After the next corner, the truck turned right and headed toward the mountains. After one block of apartment buildings and two short blocks of suburban homes, the road opened and there were only a few houses along the side. The sun was now in their eyes, so Jonathan and Mike flipped down the truck's sun visors and put on wayfarer-style sunglasses.

"Sometimes I wish I was still carefree and single," said Mike. "I could dig a trip cross-country myself."

"C'mon. You have a nice wife and kid," Jonathan said. "That's pretty important."

"Hey," said Mike. "You sure you're going to be OK to drive today.

Why don't you take an extra day and rest before you leave?"

"Can't. Damn bastards. If they would've sent me an acceptance letter earlier, I could've left last week and enjoyed the trip cross-country. As it is, I'm going to just have enough time to stop and sleep eight hours each night."

"No Grand Canyon? Damn. Can't say you lived a full life unless you spit in the Grand Canyon."

"Did that. When I was a kid."

"Guess you ain't got much more to live for then."

Jonathan laughed and turned to look out the window. There were a few scattered farms, pine trees, and some grassland.

Mike backhanded Jonathan in the chest.

"You make sure you put me in one of your novels," he said. "Ya hear?"

"O.K., bud."

The road inclined.

"Glad I won't have to deal with Fred anymore," Jonathan said.

"Fred!" said Mike, sitting straighter in the seat. "That damn bastard. I should be the senior officer, not him."

"Well, you're not living with the company owner."

"Yeah."

The truck slowed and turned into the parking lot of a single-roofed complex of six or seven ground-level offices. Fir trees loomed over the building. They drove around one end of the building and parked in back. They removed their sunglasses, got out of the truck and closed the doors. Jonathan listened. Cardinals and song sparrows were singing.

"You go that way," said Mike, pointing along the back wall to the far end of the complex. "And I'll go around front."

Jonathan walked, checking doors as he went. He headed toward a small field of thick grass and clover that lay around the corner of the building. Beyond that patch of grass was the tall fir wood. He twisted and rattled the knobs on each door. He scanned the fir trees for birds as he approached the corner of the building. There was one more door on the other side of the building. As he turned the corner, he saw the brilliant red flash of a cardinal as it flit from one tree to another.

A wall of shadow bid him halt in mid-stride. Flies buzzed around the shadow. Jonathan smelled its rank odor and saw parasites crawling on its shoulders.

Directly in front of him was a grotesquely large black bull. Its forehead was as wide as Jonathan's shoulders, its chest was as wide as if Jonathan stretched out both his arms, and its length was as long as a pick-up truck. Between the head and the tail was at least twenty-five hundred pounds of solidly packed muscle and bone.

The bull had been contentedly chewing grass and clover but stopped in mid-chew when Jonathan blundered around the corner. The bull's eyes darkened and it snapped its head up and spit out the greens. It snorted and nasal-sprayed the front of Jonathan's shirt. Its eyes were at level with Jonathan's chin. It widened the stance of its front legs.

Jonathan began to step back, but the bull snorted again and took an even wider stance. Jonathan froze again.

The bull's flat, imposingly wide head had one horn broken off, and in the remaining jagged stump was a ragged chunk of rusty sheet metal. Its forehead, cheeks, and shoulders were scarred and its ears were ripped and frayed. The hairs inside the ears and around the jowls were graying, yet its dark eyes were clear and intently focused on Jonathan.

Jonathan began to move his hand slowly, ever so slowly, toward his pistol.

The bull shook his head and pawed the earth.

Jonathan paused. Sweat ran coldly from his armpits and his body shook involuntarily.

Behind the bull was a harem of wild- looking female cows. They were calmly eating grass or lounging on their bellies chewing their cuds. One by one, they turned their heads and stared at Jonathan standing in front of the bull.

Mike stumbled around the corner on the other side of the building and stopped on his toes, almost tumbling forward.

"Damn," he said.

The bull jerked his head toward Mike. Mike gaped at the bull. The cows pivoted their heads toward Mike.

Jonathan spoke. "Use your…"

The bull yanked his head back toward Jonathan. Jonathan froze again. The cows looked at Jonathan.

Mike pulled out his baton and began to beat it on the wall of the building, yelling, "YAH. YAH. YAH."

The cows jumped, and the bull agilely spun his huge body toward Mike and lowered his head.

Jonathan ran around his corner.

The bull looked over his shoulder at the empty space where Jonathan had been.

Mike moved.

The bull charged Mike.

Mike ran around his corner.

The bull stopped.

Jonathan reached the truck and hurriedly entered the passenger side. Mike arrived a few seconds later from the other side of the building and got in driver's side.

They were out of breath.

"Shit," Mike said.

"Damn," Jonathan said.

"Shit."

"Damn."

"Shit."

"I almost died," Jonathan said.

"Me too," Mike said.

"He was ready to impale me," Jonathan said. "He could've gored and smashed the living shit out of me."

"Damn," Jonathan said. "I've never seen a bull that big."

The bull bellowed from the other end of the building.

"Neither have I," Mike said.

"He was right in front of me. Ready to kill me."

They sat there for a moment, breathing heavily, their heads in their hands.

"I think that was One Horn," Mike said.

"What?"

"One Horn."

"Oh yeah. That bull everyone in town talks about."

"I believe so."

"I thought those were all stories," Jonathan said.

"Me too. I've never seen him before."

Jonathan hit Mike in the shoulder.

"Why the hell didn't you shoot your pistol?" he asked. "He could've killed me. His horn was inches from my gut."

"I couldn't. You were right behind him from my angle. What if I would've missed?

Both paused, looking out in front of the truck at the back of the building.

"One Horn," Jonathan breathed.

"One Horn," breathed Mike.

"Jesus Christ. Ain't he supposed to be dead?"

"Yeah," Mike said. "Hasn't been a new sighting of him in three years or so. Way before you got here. They say he used to terrorize this part of the county. Used to run into the sides of trucks all the time."

"Bet that big son of a bitch could do some damage," Jonathan said. "Jesus. Did you see the size of him?"

After a moment of silence, they put on their sunglasses. Mike continued to stare at the building. Jonathan looked around. He looked over both shoulders, then checked the mirrors.

"Fred says he saw him," Jonathan said.

"Fred ain't seen anything. Fred tells tales."

"What the hell's wrong with that bull anyway?"

"You've heard the stories," Mike said. "He just ran off some farm up north and started going around running into trucks. Then he started breaking down farmers fences at night, stealing their cows for his harem. He just roamed around and did what he wanted."

"Well, I can see why. No one's gonna mess with a bull like that."

"There's even rumor that if you ever have an encounter with him, like if he runs into your truck, you run into a streak of good luck."

"What?"

"Yeah. People have won the lottery, had a windfall come their way, gotten new jobs."

"Never heard that one," Jonathan said.

"Hey," said Mike. "Let's drive around back and see if he's still there."

"I don't know if that's such a good idea, good luck or not. Did you see the width on his shoulders? The size of his head? He might put his one horn right through my door and kebob my intestines, that would be my luck."

"C'mon"

"No!"

But Mike was already starting the engine and putting the truck in reverse.

"We're in a truck, Mike. He don't care much for trucks. He…"

"Might bring you some good luck on your trip."

"Might prevent it."

The truck came around the corner of the building and stopped.

One Horn had moved closer to the wood and smelled the air. He turned to face them, lowered his head and pawed the earth.

"Mike, let's get out'ta here."

One Horn lifted his majestic head, extended his snout toward them, sniffed the air, and squinted. He held that pose for a moment or two, his nostrils wide and sucking air, his eyes squinting.

"Mike," Jonathan said.

"Just hold it a moment, this truck is big, I'll keep the front to him. Maybe he'll go for the bumper."

One Horn stopped sniffing the air and stared at the front of the truck. His eyes seemed unfocused. He looked to the right of the truck, then to the left.

Mike moved the truck a little closer.

One Horn looked quickly in the vicinity of the front of the truck. His tail swished back and forth. Then he turned away and grandeurly sauntered onto a trail that led into the wood. Each cow in turn, one behind the other, followed him.

Back at the security office, Fred, cleanly shaven and in a freshly starched uniform, leaned over the front desk toward Jonathan and Mike.

"Bullshit," said Fred. "You guys are just making this up cause it's Jonathan's last day."

Angela Farnes, the company owner, was walking around behind the desk, shuffling papers and making it obvious she was ignoring Jonathan and Mike.

"I'm telling you," Mike said. "We saw him."

"He's dead," said Fred. "No one has seen him for years. A man over in the next county says he buried him." He pointed his thumb at his chest. "I was one of the last ones to see him."

Jonathan said, "But…"

"Last truck he ever ran into was mine," said Fred. "It's a blessing. Oh, it wasn't at first, at least it didn't seem so. Had to buy a new door and side panel for my truck. Then I lost my farm. Then my wife died. But then her mother who was still depending on me for support died." He leaned closer toward Jonathan and Mike and cupped one palm around his mouth, jerking his other hand and thumb behind him, "And look what I have now."

Jonathan and Mike gaped unbelievingly at him.

Fred drew back and said, "What you guys want, a newspaper story? A bonus? You wanna drag my security business into this. No one's gonna believe you. One Horn's dead. I ain't gonna back you. People ain't gonna believe you when you say you saw a dead thing walking."

"Maybe he's not dead," Jonathan said.

"He's dead alright. And dead things don't rise."

"Forget it, Fred," Mike said.

Mike walked out the front door.

Fred stared obstinately at Jonathan. Jonathan, returning the stare unyieldingly, took the pistol out of its holster, pointed it at the sand-filled barrel next to the front desk, pulled back the slide and checked the chamber. He set it on the desk in front of Fred. He pulled out the baton from the ring on the other side of his belt and set that next to the pistol. Then he unbuckled his security belt and set that next to the baton. He extracted the two clips from their holder on the belt and emptied the rounds, counting thirty in total. He removed the shirt with the security crest on it and folded that over the weapons and belt. He stood in a black T-shirt.

"You have my last check?" Jonathan asked.

He went to the back office. Jonathan tapped his fingers on the desk. Angela looked at him out of the corner of her eyes, smiled, then winked at him. Jonathan stopped tapping.

Fred returned. Angela looked down at the papers on the desk.

"Here," said he.

"Thanks," Jonathan said as he turned to leave.

Fred watched Jonathan as he opened the front door.

"Don't think you're gonna be blessed now," yelled Fred. "Just 'cause you say you saw him."

Mike was looking at Jonathan's black and chrome Harley Springer.

"I've always liked this bike," Mike said. "It's clean and sleek. No gaudy emblems or fringe or studded leather. And you take good care of it. Make sure it gets to New York all right."

Mike raised his hand to shake. Jonathan grasped it.

"Don't worry about Fred," Jonathan said. "We saw One Horn. Hell of an experience. No one can take that from us."

They looked one another in the eyes, and an unspoken message of life-long friendship passed between them. They unclasped hands.

"Yeah," Mike said. "No one can take that from us."

"Don't pick up any hitch-hikers," Mike said. Then he smiled and strolled toward the building and went inside the front door. Jonathan watched the door close.

Jonathan pulled a leather bombardier jacket out of an over-stuffed saddlebag, put it on, got on the bike, turned the key, and pressed the starter button. It immediately turned over and vibrated steadily. He smiled at the familiar hum coming through the handlebars and up from beneath the seat, and he felt already free. He put on his sunglasses. Without his hands on the handgrips, the handlebars rocked rhythmically with each cycle of the pistons. He pulled leather gloves out of his jacket pocket, stretched them over his hands, grabbed the horns of the bike again, squeezed the clutch, tapped the gear lever and slowly rode the bike up to the edge of the road.

He eyed the route east, up toward the mountains, the direction in which he was about to embark. Above the ridgeline was a cerulean sky with a few billowy white clouds. He looked over his shoulder and checked the traffic to the west. The road was clear. It was going to be a nice, calm ride through the mountains, he thought. He rolled the throttle and pulled out on to the road.

Moths
By Elizabeth Harrison

Old friends like moths
dance on my eyelids
like the light on the porch,
the only sign of life at this hour,
dream curtains flailing

I'm split between this bed
and the 9th grade
disco balls, the ceiling fan whirring,
while walls and the immediate white
of my pillow, these sheets,
sinking

She opens the van door
and slams it behind us.
We don't look back,
enter a loud foyer, drunk in high heels
to the lockbox,
the key in her fingers
attached at the wrist with an old phone cord

Attached at the hip,
a mickey, a sip,
bubblegum mint in the mirror

Muffled drumbeats become songs,
louder voices
Blink. I was a sexy referee
Blink. You were a cowboy,
blonde hair, blue eyes,
sad eyes speak
a universal language

It's a strange life,
a kiss from the archives
forgotten 'till now,
a new mouth, two mouths
exchanging need like nothing.
Rewind
the lessons,
tangled patterns,
shadow bruises.
Close your eyes

These fragments unfold
fully formed as I remember them,
visceral, close,
warm bodies
stifling heat in the room
like the summer at night when it rains

Roll over the years in between;
it's like my cat knows what I need
as she crawls in my arms
to be the little spoon.

Selected Poems
By Lilian Caylee Wang

Devotions

I haven't cried lately
long enough to forget dreams of endlessness
of cockatoos, of circles
of crimson

I live quietly
as if I aged all my years in this year
I worry about roadside strays
and whether the people I pass on the street
hate me

"A colored woman's road trip"
through a country that wants me to go home
birds grow louder as you travel south
blue jays, cardinals
innocent to the carelessness of legs and elbows
wooden canes and metal guns

I run through the dusk of April
as spring's folklore
gathers around honeysuckle branches
spreads into the stillness between us
sprinkles pollen into my hair
and freckles onto my cheeks

The miles grow
so does the emptiness

and the promises of stone fruit and thunderstorms
I make a home wherever I am
wait
for sunflowers nodding their heads
morning's breath
faith
you

When I sing along with you

I have a song in me yet. I'd forgotten; I don't
touch keys anymore, and pregnant
pauses wait in the creases of our covers
the once-gentle curves of our mouths when we try to kiss
We don't sing anymore. We're left
with frozen waffles for breakfast
we peel clementine after clementine
our hands lose their meaning
counting themselves away

We left the gold behind. We escape
to salt-strewn shores
watch eight-foot waves erode our senses
we measure blood oxygen levels
feeling my heart beats

We take sugar in our coffee. We
spilled milk on the table
in the mornings we stumble
into forgotten wells of grief opened wide
and in our homecoming

return to them before we say goodnight

I have a song in me yet. I'd forgotten
in the metronome of sorrow keeping time
submerged in the saltwater of this womb
I sacrificed it in tribute and yet
I have a song in me.

Purity

i watched myself die
with the passivity of a passerby
unmoved and immobilized
i thought this time might be different
i might have found myself alive at last
or even, be witness to my own birth
is there such a thing as resurrection?
or re-birth
or rising?
after three days
or three months
of choking on my own thorns?
imagine an end to the dazzle of pain
i wonder if anything can ever be enough again

i remember when i was solid
it wasn't much but at least i wasn't wrapped up in a sleeping bag on
the balcony, crying into the stars
at least i wasn't pouring prescription pills from orange bottles into a
Ziplock bag

these days, i find myself holding the gaze of paintings across the
room
there's an incoherence to my alphabet, a dissonance to my face,
there's a thundering that won't let me bloom —
these days, i could blow away when the winter wind storms
there are faceless furies that quake inside me
lift me above the stratosphere
i can feel myself drifting apart into soft angles and golden shadows
life here has never felt the weight of living
i resent You for keeping me tethered to the ground

i whittled down thirteen years and three great love affairs into the
ridges of Your hands
salvaged scar tissue from the times i've been torn and tattered
the rest i've lost not in a great blazing fire
but in the slow ruin that seeps and stains
there is no such thing as purity
only clockwork and panic
never mind the soil in the corners of my eyes
i scrape the insides of despair
wait for redemption
 — out-believing the minute hand
and dream of wild berries on my tongue

Porcelain Faces
By Shreeya Goyal

Mother stood in the aisle, her dress rounded with a bulged stomach, bulged thighs. It starts here, with Mother being the best person I'd known — Mother in drafty dresses and circled eyes, with a voice too kind for a boy like me. It starts when she tore herself apart in this family, and crashed onto the 78, on the path to heaven. She leaned against the kitchen door the night before, watched Macy slash her arms with the only knife in the house — arbitrary lines, the ghost echo of death. I was high, and Mother stroked my sticky hair as we watched Macy cry onto her blood.

But the thing was, only four hours before Mother died, on a sickly summer of the third of June, she was alive in this state of mind that made me think she could never leave. All three of us sprawled out against the kitchen floor, as Mother moved her fat waist and fat thighs to the music of *Casablanca*, and Macy's thin figure stared at me as I blew white wisps from my mouth. Everything was still normal, and we watched the moon gamble through the slots in my blinds — Father was out fishing, and nobody else minds my smoking. Both of them only got high when they were upset — I asked Macy, 'Want a hit?' She licked the salted crackers off her fingers and crowed down with a gleaming, piqued hindrance while I spoke of some philosophical crap — everything sounded so wise when I was high. Macy scowled in the way she always scowled: mouth drowned into a singular crease, lips pulled back, the tip of her tongue smudged up — she asked, 'Why would you say that, Ben?' I shrugged and dragged the cigarette across my mouth.

There were the beginnings of sentences and the ends of words mixed into a muddle, and when I talked, white blood poured out of my mouth. Macy and Mom didn't say anything, and they stared at me while the moon cascaded into the room, and Mother's music played in my ear. Macy snorted as I blew smoke in her ear, and ran her fingers through the cuts of the knife. I told her about a girl yesterday, how she made me nervous, and Macy said, 'Ben, if a girl offers you a blowjob, man up and enjoy it.'

At something in the morning, I lost myself halfway through a thought — Macy stared at me with a hard-weight distortion, 'Finally got tired of your own voice, Ben?' My mind split across the asphalt, rotting with the smoke, and Macy's hands were fresh red, contrasted against the white skin. Her plain face stared back at me, and she said, 'Don't say anything.' I seared the cigarette against my wrist, a ligature of white wisps, and I said, 'Got tired of porcelain skin?'

If we did live somewhere else, not in this cabin in entropy where we found posters for drug dealers falling out in the sticky summer heat, where we had one of those all-you-could-eat diners, Macy wouldn't be scar-ridden in the figment of weed. We were smack dab in the gutted core of the woods, in a white-washed community, with rich boys riding their skateboards while smoking pot, girls with their hands tied all over everything— the town with rich families, where the mothers would get high along with their children. Macy was the kind of person that was too much of herself, she was too smart for this small, desolate town. She was the ring of resignation in her face, a drunken mood stumbling into the wrong sky — there was nothing to do in this small, fucked-up town but get high. She looked at my wrist. "Why would you do that?"

"It doesn't hurt," I said. "Only stings a bit, and now I've got a tattoo, like I've always wanted. Look at me being a fucking bad boy. Want to try?"

"Jesus," she said, and she wiped her hands on her skirt, only reaching the thumb line of her thighs. Macy didn't mind; she brought intoxicated guys home, only to have them stumble in the dead of the night with their spider legs only so covered with the duvet. "You're an asshole, Ben. An actual idiot."

"Why is it you two like cursing so much?" Mom called from the kitchen.

"Everything sounds so much more profound when you curse Mom," and Macy rolled her eyes at me. We used to have a joke, if Macy would keep rolling her eyes, they would fall out of her head and roll away from her. She's too smart, too smart for this town, so she ends up watching me get high, wondering how, with resignation and amusement, she ended up here. "Think about it — if you say, 'You're an actual idiot, Ben' and if you say, 'You're a fucking shithead, Ben,' it all works out the same, but it sounds better, don't you think?"

"When did you become such a wiseass, Ben?"

I smoked and smoked until my lungs were dry and my mouth was a mold of white wisps. Mom and Macy sat beside me, and we cursed out loud. At six in the morning, Father got home, and Mother made me stomp my cigarette away, reminiscent of grainy smoke on the floor. Macy left the house now, her skirt short and sandals thin — hours later, she brought home a skinny boy, with his teeth sticking out and nostrils flared wide. I could hear them through the walls. Mother and I changed our clothes, my legs thin against her fat thighs, and then we cursed one last time before Father walked through the door. He dropped the fish in the fridge, stared at us with darkened eyes, and slapped us until we had red welts across both cheeks.

The next day, Macy walked out of her room, her body limp, and watched as her skimpy boy ran out the door with his clothes scattered on the floors of Macy's room. From across the street, Macy's friends, all die-hard Catholics, watched and shook their heads — she flipped them off. She picked up her old shirt, balled it up, and threw it into her closet — pulling another out and over her head.

"Done with your fuck session?" I said, stupid and slow and still high.

"Shut up, Ben."

"You know he's going to get beat up?"

Macy laughed, shaking her head. "I know, I know that, Ben. God, do you ever get tired of hearing yourself? There's nothing else to do in this stupid town except fuck, anyway." The sun outside lined with glares of light, and the town was ink penetrating through it. Macy turned, folded her legs into her skirt, and told me, 'I feel dead,' but Macy died long before, in a trip made of capricious lines across her skin, her mind in heaven. She died in this fucked-up town, where there was nothing to do but get high, and there was fortitude, yet exhaustion in her face — Macy Benson became someone else. She glared at me as the sun glared at the lines of Earth, and my mind was shit from the drug intake — I felt empty, made of the white wisps. Mother's screams echoed from the other room, new, red welts across her fattened thighs, across her fattened stomach — I smoked and smoked and smoked.

"You're — you're just so fucking awful, Ben — awful sometimes, you know that?" Macy exhaled and dipped her head into her hands, my hands trembled from the weed. I didn't know. I felt awful, a turmoil in my stomach and it groaned through the tar of the cigarette. And then I kept smoking, and then I kept grinning.

"You think I don't know any shit at all, Macy?"

Macy spoke, finally — my eyes hazed out, slow and stupid. Outside there was a bike rack, coveted with slogans and pictures of naked girls -- the guys stared the most. I was crazy, a boy that was high and crazy, cocky — I was sixteen, sixteen. It was a deathless summer, in this whitewashed town — Macy fucked other guys, I got high, Father beat Mother. "He's hurting her to death. She's going to kill herself."

"The fuck do I know, Macy?" I say, dazed, dazed from mother's screams.

"Can — can you just stop?" Macy looked at the door, and she scowled through a vacant gaze. On Saturday nights, Macy eats at a Noodle House, where babies spit on other people's jackets, and fourteen-year-olds pulsate through the crowds acting like adults, too scared to actually smoke. She took me there the next Saturday night, and I was in the flesh of pulsating teenagers with baby spit over my clothes — Macy ordered the noodles, stood by the doorway, and watched a kid cough smoke. "I wish he would hurt us instead. Maybe he likes it, hearing her scream, hurting her like that."

After three hours, the Noodle House hadn't closed, and all the kids lay on the ground, knocked out and smelling of sweat and weed. They were a faceless crowd, I found myself in a faceless crowd. The police didn't come, and there was a girl with sticky blonde hair, her hand inches away from the phone — she had a plaster of vomit across her mouth. "Ben, you have nothing to say? Mother, she's so smart and sweet, and kind."

I paused. And then I said, "You're a lot like Dad, you know?"

"I don't understand," she said finally. She turned towards me, and her eyes roamed through the reflections of the stolen smoke — wet beads contrasting with abstract white. "What is wrong with you? I don't beat up who I love."

"Dad doesn't love us."

"Dad loves us."

I turned to her, matched my wet beads with hers, but I was smiling. "Has he ever told us that?"

Twenty minutes later, Macy had her lips pursed and skin against Father's door. She gnawed at her nails, until he took her in, and she became swallowed by the pity of screams and welts. When they both came out, Mom and Macy had bruises across their skins, and Dad's knuckles were broken. He dumped my cigarettes, left a few punches across my face — yelled and yelled, Father, and he punched and punched. All three of us looked as if sacked bags, welts across any visible surface — Macy knew now, Father doesn't love. I grinned the entire time he punched me, hands turmoil against the rose of my cheek — we once had such porcelain faces, all three of us.

The next morning, I woke and Macy stood over my room with her hands crossed, her expression twisted — I laughed, kind of bitter. She sat on the edge of my bed, I waited for Mom, but she never came. 'I need to tell you something,' Macy says, 'I need to tell you something and you're not going to like it.'

I make a joke, 'What's new?' Nobody laughed at my joke.

Mother and Father died in a car crash, on the 78. Dad was driving, they said he pushed Mom into the glass before slamming his head against the wheel. He was going fast, almost twice the speed limit, and he swerved his car until his engine caught fire — he drove them both to heaven, that man. Mom, her fat thighs and fat stomach were metal mixed into asphalt, and Father, his broken knuckles, scarred teeth were stuck into Mom's body. The car, just like that, exploded, and then everything caught fire — there's nothing left, nothing but Father's hand still against Mother's skin. I cursed and cursed and I am reminded of Mom.

"Oh my God," I whispered, and Macy traced her eyes back to me. I just grinned. "Yesterday was a terrible last day for Mother," and then I laughed. "It doesn't matter. She's dead. We're in the system now, you know?"

"What?" Macy asked.

"Mom," I said. "She's dead, and she's got Father's hand all over her, just like when she was actually here. I need to smoke."

Macy stood up from her spot against my bed. "That's awful, Ben. That's all you have to say?"

But then I laughed. "It's funny. You know, yesterday I thought there was no possible way Mom could die. And now she's dead. It's funny."

Macy paused, she blinked and her mouth hardened. She still looked like Dad — if she died there would be no reminiscence of this family, her eyes were two hard marbles. Over the next few weeks, I fell into a spider web of games. Walking into town became a chore; whitewashed, rich boys would yell at me, tugging at their golden lip rings. There was a guy, Daniel, and it was another spiraling web — he would push, I would pull, he would move his waist right into mine, and I would to him; his kiss was sweet, reminiscent of his chocolate talk. Macy didn't like him, and I didn't either, but we smoked and kissed and fucked, and watched other people call us things like 'fags' and laughed into their faces for it. On Saturday, I went to meet his parents, and he got kicked out of his house. Daniel said, the moment he was out the door, "Wanna get high?"

I drove him to my place, and Macy would stare at him like he was the setting of broken glass -- he had a cleared face too, Daniel, he had his cleared skin racked with welts. Macy baked everyone cookies except him, but he said he could taste them when he kissed me.

"Your father died, right?" Daniel said, one night. "My Dad was friends with him. He was tough, mean."

And then I smiled, laid against his chest. "He was a jackass."

"You must be so upset," he said, and I shrugged. "He was your father, Ben."

"I don't know," I murmured. "I don't know. I guess."

I rolled off his chest, and turned the other way on my bed, but he grabbed at my skin; I smiled when I pushed him off as he tried to kiss me. His lips parted like broken chocolate, and I slept in Macy's room that night. But when I woke, I was in my bed, and Daniel was bare skin against mine — Macy looked at us from the doorway with a broken glare. She played music, while Daniel and I stayed in bed the rest of the day, skin against skin.

Daniel went to college after the third week, said, "You have the best drugs, Ben." I went over to his dorm that night, the night he left, and I woke up on a couch that wasn't mine — I nudged him next to me, and we both stared at each other, he was nothing more than flesh in a skin suit. I went to his college dorm every day after, until I saw another boy in his sheets.

When I dreamt, it was of the dirtied car window I laid my head against when Daniel drove me back-- I woke up to a crash. Macy shoved around my closet, pushed all my clothes out and sifted through my dressers, knocked over my pants. She slammed my bedroom door, and walked out to the porch, cigarette held between her the slits of her fingers — we took turns searing the smoke into our thighs, where Mother's welts would be. Macy had been different then, a different person, with cigarette marks braising her thighs, hands tied around the cancer stick. She tried to speak, and stuttered — in this stupid, whitewashed town, I had lost, in Daniel's dorm room, I had lost, and in the cabin, I had lost. Macy couldn't say anything — we both burned cigarettes into our skin, and in my head, I kissed Daniel until he was nostalgia between my teeth.

"Where's your fucking suit, Ben?" Macy asked suddenly, and she dropped the cigarette to the ground. Over the next hour, Macy yelled at me, her cheeks flushed — I yelled back, I yelled until my throat was sore. I cursed as Mom did, and the words were condolence in the dark.

"I don't know, I don't fucking know," she slams the door in front of me, and the sawdust left a feeling similar to bugs on my face. From outside, Macy's catholic friends smiled at me, and then walked with their chests popped out. She drove us to the mall, and on the radio, we listened to *Casablanca.*

"We need to get it cleaned," she said, about a suit. The mall stood a standstill grey, where kids ran into each other and had smeared ice-cream over their faces.

"No, we don't. It's fine."

"I don't — you — they were our parents, Ben." Macy stood, stood with seething rage, and her figure was the glint of a knife through the dark. We both left without paying, and she ripped the cuff-link off the suit, a jagged seam now left behind. I smoked a cigarette on the way out, and a security guard punched my face — his hand was like Father's.

"Look, it's a little loose," Macy said, once we got home. The moon shone through the glint of mother's old fake china — the flowered designs with cracks in them. I had a girlfriend once, Susan, and her lips were soft, hair a plastic blonde. She tasted like bubblegum and lip gloss — she danced with me on every date, and I could feel her whole body against me. We broke up when she found me behind a barn, with my hands tied around brunette hair, and body against a skinny, petite girl; when I got home that day, I broke

Mother's china into shattered glass. "Can you hold it up? We'll get a belt."

Seventy minutes later, we arrived at the church, old and rickety against the smell of alcohol. The funeral was held on a sticky summer day, winded with guests in silk suits and thin dresses. I sat through Father John's sermon, thinking about fucking Daniel and smoking, burning holes into his skin — then, we all stood to place flowers on Father and Mother's dead bodies. Macy gave a eulogy, but she didn't cry — she said that Father was delightful and Mother was nothing less than fierce, but her eyes were wet beads and the speech was a facade of lies cascaded in the dark.

We heard apologies, for Father dying, for Mother dying, for Daniel and I, for the smell of cigarettes on the two of us — 'the only way they can make money now is by selling drugs.' I laughed when they said sorry, shook my head — Macy told them, "He's gone crazy. A little foggy in the head, because of this whole thing. Didn't have a strong connection with his father, too."

One of the ladies said, "Is it because of this Daniel?"

Macy and I stood in the hallway, watching the rich, whitewashed youth jerk off in the bathrooms and then whine to their parents about something or other. We watched Mother's sewing friends leave knitted scarfs on the caskets, and Father's fishing friends pound their hands on each other's backs. Macy held her fingers against my shoulder pads, and said, 'You look so much like Father,' but all I saw was the red on our porcelain skin.

At some point during the funeral, Macy and I stumbled into our house, high on smoke, high on the glass bottle in my hand — somewhere between stoned and drunk. We sat outside, with the liquid light we saw in the sky, and it was sometime between sunset and the next day — we threw pebbles on our neighbor's roof. 'They're just kids, what the hell do they know,' they said back to each other. We did shit; burned cigarettes on each other's legs, threw our beer bottles, used the glass shards to carve our initials onto each other — we were high and we were a slow stupid.

Daniel came over later in the night -- Macy told him to fuck off, and I glared at him, only to see the other boy tangled in his sheets. He didn't say anything, he didn't apologize, just stood at my door with a bag of weed and a cigarette curled around his lips. 'I don't need to get stoned,' I told him, and he said, 'Of course you do.' Daniel wasn't stoned, Daniel wasn't high, but he grabbed my arm and dragged me to the porch outside where I collapsed on his chest — we looked at the stars and he told me the stars didn't mean shit. When I kissed him, his skin was rough and his lips were honey-combed in apathy.

"Daniel," I purred, and then fell into his stumbling chest. "Daniel, Daniel, Daniel — Daniel and Ben, it sounds so wonderful."

"You fucking idiot, Ben," he said, but he was smiling.

And then we went to my bedroom -- he carried me up, and I fell asleep in his arms. I was suddenly aware of his skin — soft, tense and as I grabbed at it, he moved at mine. His stomach was fat in the moonlight, like Mother's, and I smoothed the hair out of his face. "Daniel, Daniel, let me kiss you."

"You're high, Ben."

It was slow, and stupid, everything. "Let me kiss you, Daniel."

Daniel's lips were slow, like tar, and his taste stumbled me into a memory. One hour before the crash, Macy traced her cigarette burns, and her skirt was short enough to see the lines of holes. My teeth pulled into a grin, and from inside I could hear father pelting against Mother's skin — she never said anything, Mother. Macy said, with wide, wet beads of eyes, "He's going to kill her, Ben."

Daniel's mouth became a dim, washed-out room, as Father tore mother with ravenous hands, deceit for those unsafe — I smoked and it seeped under his door, into the flesh of his room. When they both walked out, Mother was a kind of limp that looked as if she had all her bones broken — Father slapped me across the face, rosy cheeks in turn of white ones. 'Father, you're going to break all your own fucking knuckles,' I said. Macy stared at me with sorrow, drawn-out lips, and Father turned my face into a sludge of bruises and lesions. He took Mother by the arm, tore her apart to his car, and drove the car all the way off the highway — reports say he pushed her before they met the edge of the cliff, and the remains of his hand carved into her splattered body.

Macy and I sat in a hot car afterward, a red Honda we found at the end of a street. She asked me if I thought she would be a good mother.

"I don't know," I shrugged, and the smoke gassed the metal doors. "Not really."

She hovered at the tip of my skin, right there, and she wasn't asking a question so much as looking for her answer. Her skin shot up and her mouth drew close; I imagined Mother's blood on our car's seats.

"You really think so, Ben?" Macy's hand hovered over the silver handle of the car, burned in the sunlight.

"Yeah — yeah, Macy," and for some reason, I started laughing.

I looked at Daniel, his mouth tied into unearthing reminiscence, quiet moans that said he loved me, and I kissed his skin in gasps — he didn't understand, I don't love. When Daniel kissed me, he moved his hips to mine; all that mattered in that sultry,

July night was that there was a beautiful boy who I didn't love, who was on my bed on the night of my parent's funeral.

Daniel kissed the bruises father left — we were once porcelain faces.

Self-Portrait with the Sound of the Sea
By Lily Emerick

Rain outside, tainted
with salt like skin,
my head in your lap,
around us trees,
above us trees and fog
and that thin rain
I have heard called
pelo del gato
in jungles far south,
hair of the cat,
its lyricism lost
in translation like all
intangible things.

You are reading to me
about the clay
figure of a golem,
somnolent in his empty
apartment, never looking
out the window.
The dome of our yurt
might as well be
the pantheon
just as anything can
be art if you want
it badly enough;
as if to prove
my point the trees
crowd around the oculus,
their Doric trunks
adorned with intricate
moss relief sculptures.
In the distance,

the sound of the sea
scrapes away everything
it can touch.

You bring me offerings
of small-capped mushrooms,
wishing to soothe
its rasping hunger.
Together we pinch
their stalks, hoping
they might bruise
blue. No luck. Still
in the background the sea—
I can't help but feel
it will wash us away,
and the wreckage will
leave only empty husks:
bread bags swollen
with water, floating
tree trunks stripped
of their moss,
our own bodies
puffed and blue,
cleaned inside out
by gristly maggots,
and anything we might
call art will be left
self-consciously to rot.
All around us
thrifted poetry books
begin to decay,
the stiffness
of their spines crackling
against my hand
while the rain hisses,
plying at the roof

with its salt
-stained fingers.

Later, you undress me
in the dark,
the trees shying away
from the opening
in the wind.
Are we beautiful—
I mean could we be art?
If I say you are like
Bernini's David, with
your folded forehead
and pursed lips, hair
falling into your eyes
as you bend to kiss
my breasts? And I
am the leather of your
slingshot, arching back
to be pulled taut.
Though of course
we are not
really marble, but
something softer,
closer to fruit
our bones only waiting
to sink into the earth,
like crumpling clay
into a ball, rolling
it out to start again.

Water is seeping
through the cracks, it is
the thin-haired
rain, the salt-scrape
of the sea.

I'm not so sure
I don't want to be
washed away.
It might be easy,
your tongue
on my skin pushing
me off the shore,
the golem, in league
with Goliath all along,
leaving a vacant window
and the sea
pulling us both
away, away.

Selected Poems
By Claire Jussel

Dry Creek

Between folds of hill,

    winter sun burns burlap grass gold,

cloud turns valley into frothy sea,

    weather station anemometer casts

orbed shadow onto wind-rounded snow,

    crystalline nodules skitter like rain stick, like guiro.

In the still, saliva turns

    in the back of my throat,

birds softly *pew pew*,

    the animal growl

of a salt truck roaming the ski road

    crosses the gulch

lined with a zig-zag of carmine

    creek brush and toothy boulders

shadowed green with underbelly moss.

    Somewhere down there,

dog rose hips, blood bright, jeweled

    with dewed ice arch over glass

leaves over trickling water.

    Sometime, back in summer, wild

rose grew, grows, rabidly

even as the hill grass dries.
Somewhere down there,
        melting paths are marred deep
with muddy boot print wells,
        and somewhere down there, unknown kindnesses
of earlier footfalls compressed
        snow into ridges that became treads
across ice. Somewhere further up,
        the trail winds
to a Venn Diagram intersection
        of sage steppe and ponderosa forest.
Somewhere up there,
        redband trout survive
the creek all year, even when summer scorches
        most of the creek bed dry,
adapted to survive in sparse pools of warm,
        low oxygen water until rain
and melt grant them passage
        to the tree lined river miles below.
Sometime in the past, I didn't know I lived in a desert,
        but oh I loved what water brought:
snow, petrichor, green hills, full creek
        crossings. Sometime, back there,
in my childhood, I fell

and a thorn the same color as scrape and scab embedded

into my skin, unnoticed

    until some part of my brain took over, instructed

me to press gently on the raw skin

    on either side and it rose

back out of my knee

    in one curving piece.

Rabbits

have made a message board in the snow
behind the waterlogged bungalow
with tracks dashed
and dotted between
fence line and juniper
hedge, gray dimples
in the white multiplying nightly.
When I remember one
rabbit from my childhood,
they come up by the thousands:
white, sharp, and wriggling in the cup
of my two hands pressed together
at my great uncle's rabbit farm
where a fluffle of cousins was always
running past scraggly pomegranate trees,
chasing lizards through the rabbit shed jangling
with claws against
chicken wire, hurrying
tightrope style, one foot over
the other between rabbit dropping hills;
they papered the walls of my childhood
home, bronze hued above

kitchen cabinets, soft and round
circling the cream room, overseeing bedtime;
stories that end with the big hare saying
to the little hare *I love you to the moon
and back* read with my sister and I curled
tight to either side
of our mom before
our dad would lift us up
to the ceiling in turns to touch
the glow-in-the-dark galaxy
and we would name
them as we went
star, star, planet, moon. I keep
accidentally writing poems about my childhood.
I begin intending to write
some obtuse metaphor
about how the plumbing
in the house I live in now keeps failing
as the world keeps falling
apart and see the rabbit tracks in the snow out the window
and go bounding
towards pining for I don't know what
like I'm reaching for something to put
my finger on, to hold
against a smooth plastic version of and name
*this is a star, that is a moon
rabbit feet are for wishing
moonshots are for dreams.*
Maybe this is some revelation
or remedy I don't
understand yet or an ode
to my parents I am still learning
how to write
or maybe all these memories have tracked
in just to say
isn't it a wonderful thing?

to dwell on the small
footfalls in snow, and know
that the nut-brown bundles you see huddled
and motionless in the blue
shadow of snowdrifts spend
their night hours dancing
in the muted glow of city light
beyond the darkened windows?

Ochre Sea Star

splayed solar flare
under rock lip,
in tide pool dip, wedged

into crevices,
lining sea cave crescents
like primordial palms

pressed on desert walls,
gobsmacks of tangerine
& violet paint bright

on basalt, struck
by Pacific waves,
flesh leather & braille

bump ridgeways
like neurons like highway
lattice lit up at night,

like sunlight
hitting closed eyes illuming
inner lid vein paths, vibrant

in tidal kaleidoscope
swirl among green
anemone, purple urchin,

jawfulls of bleached teeth
barnacles, mussel beds
of indigo & onyx scales

muscling out space on substrate—
filling whole rocks & pools
with subdivisions, suffocating

other species—until
along comes sea star
prowler carnivore

macaroni tube feet hungry
hundreds gripping
holding rock to rock to

shell as sea star stomach inverts
into the opening,
devours

prey from inside
its own nacre home,
preserves balance

and varied habitat palette
with each feast—until
wasted water

corrodes too much ochre,
limbs crumble
into brine, into fevered

sea in pieces
in masses,
suns going out

down the whole coastline
of a continent,
arches between arms

disintegrating,
Pisaster ochraceous
disastrous asters losing petals

to wilt & rot,
radiant skin rusting
under tides high & hot

The Dead on Facebook
By Joshua McKinney

> "Facebook just made death a little less scary."
> —TIME magazine, February 12, 2015

> "I've got a million friends!" —Bob Dylan

Now that I can plan my digital afterlife,
advertise

the presence of the absence
I've since

stopped considering, will my serial
memorial,

overseen by a "legacy contact,"
attract

friend requests from those unknown
or those

I may have known? Will eager
strangers

like my page? Will an icon with a tear
confer

the hush of grief, quiet as the quick
click

of a mouse? Will I be forever lurking?
Networking?

     *   *   *

Perhaps it is a dogged remembrance
prevents us

from the bliss of forgotten loss,
crass

though it may sound? Memories persist,
resist

the conjugation of day to month to year,
adhere

like a bur in a sock. I feel chafed,
debased;

so when the message notification tolled,
I scrolled

through tedious posts to find a late
update

from one I knew was gone—a kind of ghost
post.

And I knew better, of course. Still
the thrill

I felt when the famous poet "accepted" me
three

days after I'd read news of her death…
my breath

stopped! The pleasure center in my brain,
inane

as it sounds, released its dopamine.
The screen

at which I'd often felt alone and abused,
proved

that there's no reward like deferred
reward.

*   *   *

And yet the awful craving soon returned,
disturbed

me with the thought that with the heartless
departed

any connection is impossible to retrieve.
The aggrieved

want news the dead cannot bestow—
like how

in hell did you freeze to death, Kevin?
Is heaven

the place you reconnoiter now
in snow,

where you can piss your final trace,
a smiley-face,

forever? Your death was like a bad joke.
Poke

me to let me know that you're out there;
share

a photo to prove there's no more pain.
And

*   *   *

I hope you will forgive me, Patricia;
my wishes

for your birthday came too late. I guess
this

poem, too, is way too late and far too slow.
And you,

Evan, when I saw your face in the feed
my need

to message you was weird. The handsome
phantom

of your profile pic still smiled,
undefiled

by time or by the crash that killed you.
I knew

it was your mom who made the post,
lost

and wracked, pitched past pitch of grief,
her faith

the last thing left to clutch. But mine is gone,
undone

by the dead trapped in the bandwidth,
sandwiched

between what someone had for lunch,
Trump's

latest tweet, or a niece's umpteenth selfie.
Help me,

Judith, to ignore the pull of social media,
the devious

whisper that the dead are still alive,
slave

still to the illusion of consensus,
endless

image streams promoting public intimacy,
vaguely

hinting that all of us can think alike.
A "like"

on Facebook is, like it or not, a tiny lie.
To say

that death is, from a marketing perspective,
effective,

may be true, but to expect return…
I've learned

to ignore the lure of that small green dot;
chat

is something the dead cannot afford.
What's more,

I rattle the keys but can't unlock the cipher
of cyber

limbo, where the dead still appear
to care

about the maintenance of their hallowed
accounts.

*   *   *

Face it, our names are written in the opaque
book

we call fate. Death—we can't escape
that cliché

it's like an invitation to some big event
we can't

ignore, one where we can finally depart,
restart

in another realm of peace and grace,
a place

where we'd all like to remain on
vacation

forever. But since there are no photos
or videos

of it, there is always a nagging unease
decease

won't be the happy virtue that it seems
in memes,

that perhaps our status won't be fine
offline.

We may end up as bone, or worse than bone,
alone.

And after all, isn't that the fear we fear
to share:

that we really don't know how it ends,
Friends?

girl with spine of water
By Samantha Ellis

The child with liquid vertebrae moves like a wave, like a river current, like rain that rolls softly off the duck's back. She flows down streets through the cracks in sidewalks, arriving at the school steps quicker than her classmates, provided she doesn't take a wrong turn and end up in a storm drain somewhere. On cold days her bones are thick and sluggish unless it's freezing. Then the waterfall inside her turns to ice and she stands straight and walks straight, moving on the world instead of through it. But the normality always ends when she sits down at her desk because even though the elementary school's heater hasn't been updated in years, it still gets warm enough to melt her, to leave her as a puddle pooled in the dip of her chair.

The summer, though, means no school which she's grateful for. The June sun turns her bones to air and she floats over the grass, the evaporated droplets of her spine desperately trying to rejoin themselves with the sky. She knows the other kids would laugh (even more than they already do) if they saw her there, suspended in air like a wayward cloud.

She is young, but not stupid. She knows that one day the gentle wake of her girl body will grow until she is a tsunami of a woman, unable to touch land without destroying it with herself.

When that day comes, she will not be surprised. She will know what happens next.

She will crash through city streets, make her way to the storm drain, willingly, for the first and only time. She will find herself in the river and follow it to the ocean. She will empty herself into the waves.

Finally, finally, she will touch the tide and become it.

mars when the war is won
By Samantha Ellis

When I came home after all those years, I was sure I would be exhausted with relief, collapsing into your arms and sleeping for days. But then you cried when I showed up on the doorstep and I should have too, but my eyes stayed dry. Later, you made my favorite meal, watched as I slipped it between cracked lips, and I nodded but didn't taste a thing.

I couldn't sleep. Not when I was next to you, and not alone either. It was all too quiet. There was a sadness to the stillness, something unnerving about the silence. It made me sit up in bed, eyes searching and desperate in the darkness. It still does, when the moon is full, the light outside aflame, like a silver torch in the underbrush of night. Everything is too easy to see, the mind plays tricks with shadows I should dread, but long to meet.

One night, wrapped in silk sheets and staring at that cold moonlight, some festering wound inside of me stung and I was forced to admit that I miss the screams, the chaos, the taste of blood in the air. I have come to terms with the fact that I do not know what to do with my life when I am not throwing it at someone's feet. There was no more room in my hands, yet there was nowhere to lay my sword down.

I never asked for sympathy, only for understanding that I am not to blame for what I am. You gave me that, in the form of seeds to plant in the garden. You forced me to juggle life and death between my fingers until one could no longer remain. On the last day of July, I buried my sword in the dirt. You held me as I cried for the first and only time when I saw them. Our flowers had bloomed, late summer roses, red as blood.

Selected Poems
By Heather Lang-Cassera

Such Small Wanderers

Not wanting to care
for the pigeons,
their patterns of negative night sky bodies,

not wanting to love
their heart-curved flesh,
too large for the dry riverbeds
of my hands,

not wanting to justify my unshadowed
tenderness for something
buoyed and overripe and understanding
of her own need,
and surrounded by silent songbirds,

not wanting two wings almost identical
in symmetry, shadows
that strangulate the ground,

not wanting invisible tongues
of perfect pink oleander
forever pressing onward
even in this arid sky—

a birth cry, a death breathing, an intangible
sun, a heap of inconsolable hope
available only from yesterdays,

these fingers become bandages
for everything
in my body that might someday be broken,

the obscurity of other blunt souls
dredges bee pollen
as bright sorrow,

horizons as weeping everything,
murmurs as fragile bundles,

anguish illuminated
in each of these
exquisite gallopings.

Delicate Enough to Be Risked

Always empty
by running, pink & bleating
with wilderness,

new homes choose
the undeniable, the forest, frenetic,
the cobalt morning. You touch them

apart from me, an unnerving
room, unidentifiable. My name
watches me.

I walk the length
of the floorboard rivers, my hand's
shadow apprehensive but
ready, silent as a sliver of sharp

paper. The possible, the darkness,
the huddled dirty at the hem,

the woodland smoke scratches
at the door, like a compass bloomed

& broken, a safety pin
no longer blanketed by wildflower
corsage, a place that
is anywhere but here—

a flock of birds, tissue thin
from where we stand,

a life, an object exposed, yet unspoiled,
mistaken & unchangeable, like someone
in grey wool socks, drenched,
coming back, to you, before winter.

Ghost Light

The nightlight keeps its sloping hum,
        an invisible sound.
A home exhales, *line*,
        rests in a dark theatre.

An invisible sound
        like empty spoon, like brimming fear,
rests in a dark theatre,
        curtains made of pink carnations.

Like empty spoon, like brimming fear,
        the storms came before morning,
curtains made of pink carnations
        tossing petals in the cold rain.

The storms came. Before morning,
      the wood was riverscape, the bicycle still.
Tossing petals, in the cold rain,
      the nightlight keeps its sloping hum.

After Everything—San Francisco
By Benjamin Faro

Change—simply a connection
bridging tenses like the Golden Gate—

was, is, will be—different when you
look at them alone—but,

together, you will see that one thing
leads to another—

breath to death—Oakland to
San Francisco, or the

other way around—nothing exists
in isolation—

pick a moment, any moment—
whether or not

you were or will be; nonetheless,
it has led to

now, or now will lead to it—say a
prayer to San Andreas,

peering into Alcatraz, and pretend that
you're a helpless

angel, who cannot free a soul with this
heavy, beating heart

that wasn't always there, knowing one
day it won't be

beating, once it is exhausted, overgrown
with visceral fat and

grief, and you can't just ask yourself,
Should I have

turned around? as you sit in traffic over
shark-infested waters—

looking west, toward the ocean—San
Francisco's orange

glow rising over unknown stories of
every kind of change.

From start to finish you recite it once
again—the prayer;

or, at least you try. Something, something,
safe and sound,

and the fog rolls slowly in.

Growing Pains
By Natalie Eckl

The oak out back
runs rings around me,
up and out, towards
light, through storm.

At eleven, I could no
longer leave my bed,
sick, chronically, left cringing
at the sound of song

as it seeped through
my window. The neighborhood
children played hopscotch,
ate hot dogs in the shade.

How unfair they look up
to leaves, can feel them fall
across their face
when the wind blows.

Notice the curvature of the spine,
a call upon the sun
to do better. I won't learn
to make such demands

for years to come,
frightened of the maker
that might resent my asking
for more, yet

how everything leans towards life,
even me calculating

risk against reward
even me, even me still.

you could be worse
By Joanna Theiss

Miniskirt evening at her new apartment, her neighbor below bangs on her floor beams, bellowing about her high heels, proboscing her optimism

> *could be worse*

> *at least she got in on an upper floor*

Her new manager's eyes are an arthropod's, sucking her in, venous. Don't you look ravishing in red

> *is that all*

> *my old boss liked to grab my ass*

Midnight, bush wicked back to the city after a clawed weekend at her parents' house on the Cape, butter loading corned cobs, bibs lobstering loaded besties—

> *must be nice*

> *am i supposed to be relating to this chick or what*

—Ashley, clammy, finds her parked car, its windows smashed, compartments metastasizing papers, proof of insurance. A violation

> *violation is a little much*

> *she has insurance*

> *(and of course her name is ashley)*

House keys shook, scritching on lock, unreasonable to think, has the violation prolonged indoors, waiting up for her, waiting under her sheets

let me guess

no one was in ashleys house

Next day, hand-heated cell phone, into which the biopsying doctor smears her results while Ashley watches window repairman web out her windows

that was quick

usually those guys take forever to come

Ashley, you do not have a cancer that has crawled into bones, lungs, brain, blowing holes in matters and swells in masses. Ashley, your cancer is pluckable, removable, a mere scissoring out of your uterus which you have not utilized anyway

well that sucks

but it sounds like a not-bad cancer to have

and see what i said about insurance, no doubt this girl has *health insurance*

Find Ashley needled up, veined under with anesthetizing chemicals. Ashley, slacked dozing during surgery, a surgery when a rare complication of sedation complicates the rarity of cervical cancer in a woman so young

meaning

Meaning, Ashley does not wake up from Ashley's hysterectomy.

huh

well

could have been worse

at least she got out while she was under

Selected Poems
By Alexander Lazarus Wolff

Belle Isle

When you first saw the man, you remembered walking
with Jonathan on Belle Isle, remembered the derelict hydro-
electric plant and how the ear shut like a clam, resisting
the river's roar and the rustling of the wind-
ripped trees. You watched the combers
break on the fragmentation of rocks
running alongside the trail as the frenzied man
darted down the path only to rebound back to the start
like a bullet in a chamber.
                The mind does strange things.
And the imagination transfixes with thousands of images.
You walk down Reserve Road, and you fear
someone will rob you, you peer into the mirror
and see someone else. The man watched his wife
fall into the river. Her foot slipped on the rocks,
and she toppled, cracking her skull on the way down,
and the waves rose to swallow her, sweeping
her away as the man screamed and screamed.
There was September's mist clinging to your skin
and the scent of the moist mulch at the roots of trees
as darkness dropped down from the sky like a damnation
because you couldn't comfort the man
when he threatened to kill himself, and because
his eyes were widened to a whiteness,
and because he ripped off his shirt out of distress,
as he leaped off the edge into that dark water
full of unnamable things.
                The next morning,
two park rangers found their bodies on the shore
to the south of the island.

The Blue and the Black

The sky a sea of black liquor.
The stars regarding me sadly.
The cars shining their headlights of artificial amber.
The people walking about, engaged with each other's presence.
The cacophony of the crowd's voice turning into a whirl.
The stars piercing through the night's carbon paper.
The sky morphing into a mauve, swallowing
each dot of light, before thinning to blue-grey.
The tatters of clouds are frayed like threadbare clothes.
The sun a scorching orb, burning the grey from the sky.
The blue flattening and flattening.
The speck that is me recessing into the cityscape:
a light drowned out and as forgotten
as a box in the attic.

Having It Out with Anorexia

> *"We turn skeletons into goddesses and look to them*
> *as if they might teach us how not to need."*
> *— Marya Hornbacher, Wasted: A Memoir of Anorexia and*
> *Bulimia*

1 The Disordered Senses

The delusion is of purity:
a promise to purge
the self of its contaminates,

flaying the body
of fat and flesh, carving
it down to each sinew.

Anorexia

was my anesthetic.
What pain could penetrate

that cage of half-
truths and self-denials
in which I locked myself?

Fat was heretic.
Now, there is skin
stretched taut over razor-

like clavicles, the empty
bowls of my hip bones.
I am starved and sinless.

I have given myself
to the enemy, eaten the enemy,
have swallowed its mantra:

it feels good not to need.
To be thin
was to transcend.

2 Binging and Purging

But the body, out of starvation, betrays the mind:
three packets of cookies, a cake, a large pizza,
cereal, brownies, two sandwiches,
a dozen doughnuts, fried chicken, candy bars.

I would tear off the cellophane wrapping,
and shove handfuls of food into my mouth
only to vomit it into a garbage bag seconds later.

3 Advice from a Friend

"Why can't you just eat?
One day won't cause you to gain weight."

4 Walking

I would walk miles of tarmac, passing
each dim streetlight in the decaying dusk.
Though my muscles were atrophying—
a pain pulling at each leg— I didn't care.
At least I was losing weight.

5 At One Point

At one point, only a few years ago, I saw
suicide and self-destruction as something chic,
an ornament for the self.

I was 95 pounds, mired in depression
and the hospital, shivering under a paper-thin blanket.

The orderly would rattle up the hallway
with her metal cart, the plate, with its 600 calories
of Salisbury steak, shuddering next to the scalpels and forceps.

How long I was in that hospital room and its sterility —
the fluorescent lights stinging my eyes
with their hygienic flare; the telemetry clinging
to my ribcage; the IV bag pumping

electrolytes into my veins. I still recall
the weightiness of the magnesium
rushing into my veins, flooding my blood
like a viscous metal.

6 In the Morning

My mother would hover over me as I slept
to make sure I was still alive.
I wonder how many hours she spent
attentive to each twitch, attuned
to the risings and fallings of my chest
that signified life.

7 A Ripple

A skeleton wore my clothes,
the XS-sized shirt hanging
from clavicle and collar bones
as if from a clothes rack.
It is tired of trying.
It wants to be left alone,
left out in a charnel ground
where vultures can peck
at the flesh, and the sun
dissolve it to ash.

We move on to my twentieth
therapist. And I feel
relieved of myself, the buzzing
of my psyche quieted,
and inside me the stillness
a pool of water possesses
just after a rock was tossed into it.
The ripples disbanded, fading
out to leave a surface as placid as glass.

Gradually, I came back to friends,
to books and poetry; came back
to the taste of an orange's zest.

8 *Three Years On*

Anorexia and bulimia, your masochism
will lie latent, waiting in the space
between each synapse.

Neurotic and self-sabotaging, you'll whisper
to my psyche, seizing me with your onslaught
of numbers, and turn me into someone obsessed
with the calories in my coffee's creamer.

Three years and twenty-five pounds removed,
I finish my breakfast and step outside,
into midmorning's mild gold. September's mist
settles on my skin, and I sense

a quiescence of mind.
How remarkable is this morning:
the bronze of dawn cresting over the horizon.

Spare Me My Future
By Claire Scott

Some store memories in boxes
tight in the attic,
next to sepia photos
and dusty strollers
or in locked in closets
with moth-balled coats
or chained like Houdini
and tossed in a lake
memories of hands insisting
a moist mouth stinking of beer
but memories stalk their sleep like stilts
of lightening or rise wet from the river,
chains clanking

I stored memories in the future,
kicked them down the road
like Pelé, a soccer ball
that never happened
that never could have happened
I slept soundly at night
but now the future is now
memories in straitjackets
covered in seaweed slime
blink in the bright light
like a game of Red Rover
my name is called over
a dead uncle very much alive
and every second I walk into
he is waiting
with chocolate promises

Flames and Other Fires
By Meg Zukin

Last summer I moved to San Francisco. In September our building caught on fire. House fires are cinematic. They happen on screen, not next door. California wildfires also seem distant until the flames are licking your stairwell. The electrical fire on Waller Street happened on the same day the sky turned Bladerunner orange in the Bay Area. A building fire igniting in the background of an unparalleled pandemic and coastal wildfires is a 2020 subplot of biblical proportions. That morning, my boyfriend John and I were driving up the 280 and back into the city after spending the night at my parents' house in the suburbs. I remember rolling the window down and up and back down again, convinced that my car windows were tinted. I remember thinking "Wow, this looks like an Instagram filter," which is when I knew my brain was really broken.

I was working on the couch, hours later, when I heard it. The alarm was just a faint beeping until it was blaring. I was lost in my subconscious then ripped right back into reality. There was no alarm, and then it was all I could hear. I opened the door and saw a neighbor tearing down the stairs, clutching his MacBook for dear life. Later, on the street, he told me the only thing he took was his "livelihood," gesturing to the device. I shouted at John, that there was a fire. I didn't know what to grab.

In California, they teach preschoolers how to read while instructing them how to stay safe during a natural disaster. Stop, drop, and roll. Crawl under your desk and protect your neck. Bring a box of Clif bars and a first aid kit on the first day of school. Just in case. For Christmas last year, my parents gave me an emergency preparedness backpack, fully stocked. This state is synonymous with chaos and catastrophe. It's still the wild west and transplants are still searching for gold in the form of top billing and bitcoin. I didn't have active shooter drills while I was growing up, but they were all I could think about when I worked from a high-rise in Los Angeles. *Where would I go?* I thought, panning the newsroom while working on yet another story about yet another newsroom getting shot up. We are at war with ourselves and don't even have time to process it.

Where would I go?

Outside the air quality was hazardous at best, fatal at worst. The wind streams and air flows from miles north spread throughout the skyline, coating the clouds with a dusty orange haze. This pollution wasn't from our fire, but two others — the Creek Fire and the North Complex Fire — that were raging. Earlier in the day, I dutifully retweeted journalists on-the-scene, who were live posting from the angry flames eating the coastline, and donated to first responders and families alike all while remotely doing my media job and pretending like everything was fine.

What would you grab in a fire? Passports, N95 masks, a custom framed photo that I spent $300 on during a depressive episode, John's birthday gifts, Prozac, two beanies, a stray pair of underwear, keys, my work computer and charger—all jostling in a giant blue Ikea bag. What I didn't grab: my wallet, journals, a vintage leather jacket, dog food, real pants, an iPhone charger, Xanax, any of our art, the two designer things I own, or my toothbrush. John fled taking only his computer, phone, keys, wallet, a pair of dirty pants and our dog.

Fire trucks came roaring around the corner, adding to the regular fanfare of the neighborhood. Haight Ashbury is nowhere near the hippie haven it once was, but people still pretend. A collection of neighbors stood across the street, watching the flames guzzle the building next door before hopping onto ours. One woman went from person to person, insisting anyone could wait inside her house around the corner. It would have been helpful if she wasn't so nosy. I texted my family as my phone battery continued to drop down.

There's a fire.

In our apartment building.

Well, next door but it might be in ours.

No, not a wildfire.

A regular one, I guess?

Yes, we're fine.

I posted a photo of the firetruck on the scene to my
Instagram story before checking Citizen to see additional footage of
the damage. I already told you that my brain is broken.

These wildfires didn't exist in the background of my
childhood. The news pegs I remember include the woman who
found a finger in her chili at Wendy's and Britney Spears' 55-hour
marriage, not an entire season dedicated to inferno. Disasters
happened to other people, on the other end of the line, on the other
side of the screen. I forgot I had ordered dinner before the fire alarm
started blaring. Rewarding myself for making it through the day.
The delivery driver was trying to figure out how to drop off the food
since the street was blocked off with caution tape. He handed off the
bags of hot Thai. Gig economy meets force majeure; truly
apocalyptic shit. With nowhere else to go, John and I trudged up
Clayton to eat in his car, where we could at least take off our masks
without fear of inhaling toxic air. Our dog climbed over the center
console and we let him wedge his way into the middle. We passed a
plastic container of to-go cocktail back and forth, taking sips like it
was a chalice and we were in church. All while the fire raged on.

I'm terrified. In general, and of the future. I don't want my
home state to go up in flames. I don't want the roads to split open,

swallowing cities whole. I don't think I could live anywhere else. Plus, where else do we go? Every place is being ravaged by disaster: natural or otherwise.

I am from California. My parents are from California. My grandparents are from California. This state — of mind, of being — is in my blood. It's part of me and it is me. Maybe everyone feels this way about the place they grew up, but I know what it's like to grow up on the edge of the world. Then have that world dismantled, simultaneously, by the future and past.

An hour later, we made our way back down to join the neighbors gathered across the street. I handed out extra KN95 masks, not knowing if people should wear them because of the disease or because of the air quality. The people next door were learning that their apartments were likely destroyed. Someone's cat was missing. My phone died and at some point we started drinking. It was like tailgating, and the most social interaction many of us had had in months. When we got back into our apartment, we traipsed through the ash and debris that coated the stairwells. There was a big pile of burnt belongings on the sidewalk. Someone moved a machine into our bedroom to suck the moisture out of our walls and another machine into our kitchen to purify the dehumidified, dry air. After a week of this, we started searching for a new apartment. Still, the wildfires raged on.

I know the curves of the 280, the standstill of the 405 and the 10 and the 110 (and the 101, and the 1). I know the slopes of the mountains, both in winter and summer. I know that the coldest winter is a summer in San Francisco. I know the Golden Gate Bridge is a rust orange. I know Weed, California and how my dad threw away the shirt I got from a gas station there when I was 16, even though he secretly smoked more weed than any other dad I knew. I know Modesto as more than just a location for American Graffiti. I know that you can get garlic fries at the McDonald's in Gilroy. That if you leave 5 minutes before the last bell you can get to Santa Cruz in 20 minutes. But after that, it will take you at least an hour. I know the glassy water at Los Gatos reservoir, the choppy waves of the Bay. I know wine country and apple orchards and how to cut over from the 5 to the 1 to make a pit stop in Carmel before getting home.

I feel deeply connected to my grandparents and our shared senses of adventure, of urgency. Moving westward. My parents were born and raised here, but they've never left — and why would they? Nobody dreams of moving to Ohio. I left for 18 months before running back as fast as I could, overcorrecting this stint in the snow by fleeing to the desert. I toured Syracuse University in the spring, which was mistake number one. They warned about the lake effect snow, but all I saw were blooming cherry blossoms and storied buildings covered in vines. I saw the campus through ivy-colored glasses. It looked just like the boarding schools I read about in YA novels. My east coast love affair only lasted so long. I remember trying to clean off someone's ice-coated windshield with a credit card and my "happy lamp" did nothing to alleviate my seasonal depression. One week of a harsh winter taught me that Native Californians and upstate New York do not mix.

I healed in the desert. Like a lizard basking on a hot rock, I soaked up the sunshine and raised my internal temperature. I traded my snow boots for Birkenstocks and spent my days lazy and lounging. I loved learning but was sick of school and spent all my extra time driving into Los Angeles to experience "real life," which at the time was dive bars and underpaid internships. L.A. is not a cultural wasteland, but an alien experiment. Its seasons are dictated by awards shows and Santa Ana winds. The city is like its state: An elliptical place, moving but not changing. Falling into repetitive pattern and motion. Living in California means constantly going up and down and back and forth. Leaving but not going anywhere. Running in place. Being on the forefront of everything new and changing, but always at the mercy and precipice of a major shake-up. One earthquake or wildfire away from being jolted back into the past, one bad IPO from dreams being shattered. California is quick and changing, but when experienced slowly, feels like more of the same on repeat. It's seducing and tantalizing, dangerous, luring in those who can handle it, as is the internet and its darkest corners.

The fires here are fast-moving but long-lasting, leaving years of damage in their wake. I am a fire.

Selected Poems
By D. Walsh Gilbert

Poet in a Long White Gown
 after *Ill Omen*, Frances Macdonald (Scotland) 1893

When the hours elongate like thin arms,
I pause among white birches.

Fast dark birds flee by, single file,
and then, leave me solitary.

I clasp my hands.
My bare feet crush moss and purslane.

I try to walk away from isolation,
and yet, a purple aura follows me.

Call it
trepidation, cowardice.

Once, I wanted to dive from a canoe,
but the lake's water was too swampy.

Once, I wanted to pick red raspberries,
but bees hid within the vines and thorns.

Once, I wanted to perch on a trap rock ledge
as if then I would grow falcon wings   and never fall.

Now I'm middle-aged,
I cut my long hair manageably short.

And, when I pause, squall-buffeted, I fear
I may not start again.

My arms dangle and my shoulders slump.
And I pray for distance from black ravens.

But I'm envious—they fly like the intrepid arrow
I still want to load and shoot.

Bows Beads Birds
—Frances Macdonald MacNair (Scotland) c. 1910

Birthed soft, winds over the pond
harden the newborn dragonfly's wings.
Nacre layered on a grain of sand
guards the oyster's inner soft—
the mother of its pearls.

And at some time,
maybe between first and second grade,
maybe between first and second husbands,
our inner little girls
who want to be pretty
—all good-girl
with watery puppy dog eyes
and pink bows tied perfectly—
focus,
learn to spread
their hidden cockroach wings
and crawl from under the baseboard.

The younger me dressed as a princess
for All Hallows Eve.
Now, I'm sorceress and choose
my paper maché mask each day.
I might be
the Carnevale's Dama or Jester.

I could be
the trickster Colombina, that pretty, little
servant girl, pure and vulnerable.
You wouldn't see the real me coming.
When I unbutton
my cape and let hungry raptors loose
like souls escaping Purgatory,
you'll be expecting turtle doves.

I am a cage, in search of a bird—Franz Kafka

after ***Enfant écrivant***, Henriette Browne (France) 1874

The birdcage door
           swings   open.
  A captured   finch
escapes.
            The question   is:
            Should we fill the coop again?

With a parakeet?
     a falcon?   swan?
   an albatross
          with a mouth   full of fish?
Do you believe
      the same bird   will return?

Must we stay empty   of possibility?

       *

A schoolgirl at the kitchen table prints her composition into a ruled book until she's interrupted—a word misspelled, dull pencil lead, a little brother spilling juice. Starting over's more difficult each time.

Then, she gives up, ragged edges of the pages torn out and left—
wadded sheets pushed away.

                    *

No matter
            how many times
you try   to   erase
      that graphite   word,

it leaves   a shadow,   or
            an impression   in the fibers

of the paper: a scuff mark,   fingerprint,

the wingflap   of venture.

Selected Poems
By Maria Crimi

A Stone in My Cheek

I have kept a stone
For years just inside my mouth
Keeping me from speaking up
Keeping me from enunciating clearly
Tasting like brine and iron
Sucking on it, instead of a thumb
Tucking it in my cheek
Knocking on my teeth, creating decay.

Prepubescent, in a two piece
I swam through the brown silty water
Of the canal, past a blinking snapping turtle,
To the bottom and opened my mouth
To let it fall out. Then
Turned in the water, struggling to find purchase
In the black muddy gunk,
I shot myself back to the surface,
Gasped for air in the sunlight
As a crow flew by and
Dropped the stone into my throat.

A tough mean teen
I'd snap it like gum
More poisonous than cigarettes
With more consequence than Mr. Rosenlicht
Who called me cunning and devious

It caused disfigurement
As it got heavier and harder to hide.
My mother cried to stand up straight.
I tried leaving it on her kitchen table
Sitting beside my father's cup
Of muddy coffee.
Brushed away like bread crumbs,
It barely left a blemish.

I tried to hide it behind my gapped front teeth
As a mother and a wife
Taking pains to check my children's cheeks.
Worrying it with my tongue
Too often biting down and
Cracking a molar or
Cutting the flesh inside my face.
Choking on it while drinking wine,
I vomited in the linen closet
Stone and teeth and flesh and blood
Spilling over white sheets and diapers.

Since then, it has sat between
Me and the stone blasters
On low coffee tables
Tumbled around and around
Smoothing its sides
So it won't cut as much
Told to leave it on my father's gravestone,
Slip it into my mother's ashes.
I tucked it behind my tongue instead
Unable to upend a cemetery.

But now I'm heavy and weary
My back is bent
My shoulders bowed
My shins splintered under a weight
That has carved and disfigured me.
So here I am, trying to spit it out
Put it in a slingshot
And put out your eye.

Super Moon

It showed up New Year's Day
in ten-degree weather
At the Dover Train Station parking lot
Over amputee city trees
With limbs sliced off for the sake
Of snaking telephone wires.
Still, quite beautiful, the moon,
Dusted, behind a haze of something.
Maybe moisture, probably pollution.
I will let you know tomorrow
How I did today. This is all I can offer
For resolution. One half-
Century has proven
That more would be fruitless,
A falsehood, a lie. Perhaps if I pay
Attention to the earth,
The phases of the moon
The solstice, the seasons.
Or a religion, a Catholic's calendar,

The year of the dragon,
Or wait till Rosh Hashanah
And start over again. Would it matter?
Me and most everybody
Have about two weeks in us
A month at best, a full moon's cycle
With a face that never turns on us,
That pulls at our fluids, and rotates
Around the earth. Super
Moon. Blue Moon. Wolf Moon.
They're coming this year,
Present, attending seminars,
A speaking gig here and there.
On "The importance of showing up."

The Gold Crestliner
By Alison Mehrman

The room was brown and small. There were no windows and
no pictures. Ma woulda hated it. Nancy, too. It was her turn next,
they said. The cop in charge, Detective Miller, kept asking me the
same things he asked last time—where I live, what I do for work,
"the easy stuff" he kept saying. None of it was easy for me.

I cracked my knuckles and started again. "My name is
Charlie Clark. I'm 30 years old, and I live with my sister Nancy and
my boss—well, her husband, Richard."

"And where do you work, Charlie?"

"At the salvage yard."

"Young's Salvage Yard?" he asked.

"Yes."

"That's Richard's business, isn't it?"

"Yeah."

"And now your family business, in a way."

I shrugged. Ma didn't like when Nancy first started dating
Richard. She always asked why a man would buy the cow when he
could get the milk for free. I didn't see how that made much sense. I
buy a gallon of milk at the store on the way home from the diner
every Saturday, and I know it costs exactly $1.06.

Anyway, it would upset Nancy, and then they'd fight. After Ma died a few years ago, Richard did marry Nancy and they moved into Ma's old bedroom. I heard someone at the diner say it was probably the money that changed Richard's mind. I thought it was just because Ma wasn't around anymore.

"How long have you worked at Young's Salvage Yard?"

"Ten years last month. Never missed a day."

"Very dedicated worker, I see. I suppose you're very important." Detective Miller grinned at the other cop as he wrote. "Now, how's a guy like you hold a job that long?"

A guy like me. I could tell he was really asking, "How's a retard like you hold a job that long?" Ma always said it was a shame, how two minutes without breathing gave me a whole life like this.

After Richard moved in, he told Nancy to stop mothering me, and she told him she promised Ma. Sometimes I call her Ma without even knowing it. One time, Richard got mad and asked Nancy if that made him my father. He was my boss first. Then my brother-in-law. He didn't want to be my father too, he said. Well, I didn't want him taking care of me anyway. He could be real mean.

"And you were working there on the morning of Friday, March 6?" Miller asked.

"Yes. Like I said, never missed a day."

"What are your responsibilities at Young's Salvage Yard?"

"I crush the cars, clean the office," I answered. "Whatever Richard asks me to do."

Miller raised his eyebrows and looked over at the other cop. "Charlie, I need you to be very clear when you answer this question, ok? Did Richard ask you to crush a gold 1951 Ford Crestliner on the morning of March 6?"

"Yes."

Ma always told me to be honest, ever since that day I lied about the dog, the one I found at the park. I thought he could be my friend, named him Rusty—I think it was from a book Ma read to me. But when I held out my hand to pat him, he bit me. I didn't really mean to, but I kicked him pretty good, and he didn't move after that. When the neighbors called and Ma asked me if it was true, I said no because I didn't want the paddle. I got it anyway.

"And did you know at the time that Ms. Davis's body was in the trunk?"

I was sad to think of her like that. Maria had been my friend since she moved here last year.

"'Course not. Maria was always real nice to me. I walk to the Downeast Diner up Main Street every Saturday for lunch, and she was one of the waitresses there. Always gave me extra jimmies."

Maria wasn't like the other women in town. She had a red apron and red lips, and she wore a shiny gold locket around her neck that Nancy said went nice with the shiny gold Crestliner she drove into town. She was real pretty, like the girls I saw in the movies. Nancy and I thought she belonged in a fancy dress in Hollywood near all the lights and palms trees. "I'll never understand why she didn't go to California or something instead of another small town in the middle of Maine with us," she said.

We didn't know why Maria chose Howland instead of Hollywood, but I was glad she did. She'd come over to my booth every week and ask, "How are you, honey?" When so many people call you retard, slow, and simpleton, honey sounds extra nice. Then she'd ask, "What can I get you—the usual?" and she'd bring me my hamburger and fries and a scoop of coffee ice cream at the end with extra jimmies.

"I see. I love jimmies too, Charlie." Miller sighed and set his pen down. He leaned in close over the table.

"Now, you need to understand why I'm so interested here. I have the body of a dead pregnant woman in the trunk of a car that was crushed at a salvage yard with only two employees. That means either you or Richard must know something. What do you know, Charlie?"

I hated answering the same questions over and over, thinking of Maria like that over and over. I squeezed my hands together and repeated what I already told them: "Richard told me to crush the car, so I did."

I thought back to the first time Maria ever came to the salvage yard. She said she was thinking of selling her car to the yard, didn't have the money to fix it at the garage.

"Charlie!" she said, closing the door to the office behind her. "I didn't know you worked here."

I smiled, set the mop back into the bucket, and straightened up. "I do. Almost ten years and never missed a day."

"That's wonderful," she said, holding onto her handbag in front of her. "I guess we haven't had a chance to talk much at the diner just yet. Maybe one of these Saturdays I can clock out a little early and sit and join you."

"That'd be nice," I said. I liked the idea of sitting with Maria.

That's how my Saturday trips to the diner started getting longer. After her shift, Maria would sit with me and eat her own ice cream—she liked mint chocolate chip—and we'd talk. She asked me all sorts of questions about Ma and Nancy and whether I was ever married or had any kids. No one ever asked me questions like that before. No one ever thought someone like me would even think about things like that. But I do. Anyway, I told her no. It had always just been me and Ma and Nancy, until Ma died anyway. She said she was sorry to hear that.

Miller sighed again. "And did you know that it was Ms. Davis's car?"

"Yes, Richard said to crush it because she sold it to the yard."

Maybe Miller didn't know why Maria needed to sell her car. She told me she wasn't making much money at the diner. She was divorced, and she didn't have anybody to help her. No family or anything, and her parents didn't give her any money like Ma left me and Nancy.

"I kept this," she said, holding the small gold locket around her neck. "My ex-husband gave it to me. Then just a couple years later he gave me divorce papers. Isn't life funny?"

I didn't think it was all that funny.

"I gave my wedding ring back, but he let me keep the locket and the car. I'd hate to sell either one, Charlie, but I might have to." She was quiet a minute and then smiled. "I don't have too many wonderful regulars like you leaving me such nice tips."

I felt bad. I always had enough money because of the salvage yard and because Nancy goes to the bank for me and leaves it in an envelope in my nightstand. She says I earn it, so I can do what I want with it, except for what Ma left us since that's all at the bank.

I told Maria I could leave her bigger tips. "Oh! No, Charlie, I couldn't ask you that. That's sweet of you, but I couldn't take your money," she said. "But," she paused, "maybe a loan instead? And then I can pay you back. Would that be alright? Maybe just $25 or so to help with the car?"

I gave Maria $25 the next Saturday. I was happy to help a friend. That was our friendship: extra jimmies and extra help. We were good friends. I hoped that maybe someday we could be more. Like those love stories I saw at the movies every week. I dreamed of pulling her in close, of her saying, "Oh, Charlie" and kissing me. I never kissed anyone before, but I figured I'd seen enough movies I could figure it out.

"Do you know how Maria got in the trunk of the car, Charlie?" Miller put his pen down on the yellow paper.

I closed my eyes. "No."

He looked down real fast. I think he heard my knuckles crack under the table.

"Charlie, what do you know about Richard and Maria's relationship?"

"I think they were good friends."

Miller sat up straight and tapped his finger on the other cop's notepad. "What makes you say that?"

"She'd come by the yard and they'd spend time in the office together."

I didn't want to think about all those time Richard told me to just get back to work.

"I see," Miller said, leaning closer. "And did Richard ever say anything about her to you, about how he felt about her?"

"No."

"And how did you feel about Maria, Charlie?"

"Well, like I said, she was always nice to me at the diner. We were friends."

And we were for a good while. She needed some more money and that didn't bother me one bit. She told me all about how much I was helping her and what a good friend I was. I started calling her every Tuesday after work so we didn't have to wait until Saturday to talk. But Nancy didn't like that. She wanted to know why the envelope in my nightstand wasn't as full and what Maria wanted with me. She didn't understand Maria just wanted to be my friend. I had to start walking down the street to the payphone just to talk to her.

That went on for a little while until the last time I talked to Maria at the payphone. It was starting to get cold out, and I was shivering pretty good by the time I put the dime in and had the phone to my ear. I pulled the piece of notepaper from my wallet and dialed the number.

"Hi, Charlie," she answered, but she didn't sound like herself.

"Hi, Maria. The weatherman said we might get the first storm of the year soon."

She didn't say anything back about the snow. "Charlie, I'm sorry."

"Sorry for what? I can help you shovel when it comes."

"It's not the storm, Charlie. It's that I—I can't be friends with you anymore."

I didn't understand. My hands started sweating.

"You know I never wanted your money, Charlie. I never asked for it. You offered. And now that I really need it, you're not giving me as much as you promised, as much as I'm counting on. It's like you don't want to be my friend after all."

My face felt hot, and I was losing my grip on the phone. "Please be my friend, Maria, please. I'll get the money. I'll get it!"

All of a sudden, Nancy grabbed the phone from my hand.

"Maria? This is Charlie's sister, Nancy. Listen, I don't know where you get off thinking you can take advantage of my brother, but I'm not stupid and neither is he," she yelled and hung up.

"Charlie, you don't pay people to be your friend, you hear me?!" She was pointing her finger at me. "That's not what you're working so hard for. People don't have to call you a retard to be mean to you, Charlie. You know better than to let someone take advantage of you."

But Maria wasn't taking anything from me; I was *giving* her the money. "You're always telling me what to do, Nancy!" I yelled and pushed her out of my way. "I'm not a little boy. I'm a man! I can do what I want. Maria's my friend!"

Nancy followed me home yelling my name, but I didn't turn around. I shut my bedroom door, threw my jacket on the floor, and walked around my room, wondering how Maria was going to get by without me and if she'd still be my friend. I really hoped Nancy didn't ruin it.

*   *   *

Miller was playing with the pen in his hand. "Ok, you and Maria were friends. Did she ever tell you anything about her relationship with Richard?"

"No, we didn't talk about Richard."

The last time I saw Maria at the diner, we didn't talk about anything. It didn't help that Nancy came with me. Maria was real cold to us and didn't call me honey.

"Charlie, you aren't going to be friends with her anymore," Nancy said real soft, eating her clam chowder. "I'm sorry, I'm just trying to take care of you, to look out for you—"

"I can look out for myself, Nancy," I tried to tell her, but she just poured a packet of Sweet'N Low into her iced tea and kept talking.

"People aren't always nice. You're going to keep your money, and from now on you won't say one more word to her beyond 'I'll have a hamburger and fries,' you hear me?"

I looked over at Maria. She was smiling at the other people as she set down their plates, the same way she used to smile at me.

"Ok, well let me ask you this then," Miller said. "You see, there's something else interesting about this case, Charlie, something missing. Everyone who knew Maria says she always wore a gold locket, but we didn't find one on her body. I need you to think real hard. Have you seen a gold locket, at the yard somewhere? Maybe at home?"

"No, sir, I haven't seen it. But I can look." I put my hands back in my pockets.

Miller rubbed the back of his neck. "Charlie, now I know you're not stupid. I know there's more to you than people think, right? So you must know I've already talked to Richard."

"Yeah."

"And I'm not saying he did, but I am saying that it would be very easy for Richard to tell us if he knew something about you, something that could make you look bad." He paused. "I want to give you that same chance—to keep it fair, alright? Do you think Richard might have had any reason to want Maria dead?"

'Course I knew Richard had a real good reason. Maria was pregnant, but they already knew that from what they did to her body. They told me it was called an autopsy. I didn't like to picture it.

I found out Maria was pregnant on a Thursday. On Thursdays, I leave work early and Richard closes up the salvage yard.

This time, Richard said he would be extra late. Nancy took some dinner over to him and saw Maria's car, and when she got back home, she was *mad*.

"That woman is unbelievable," she said, slamming the front door. "Now she's trying to get to you at work? Jesus. Richard said she was only there to sell her car. I'm surprised she would need to after all that money you gave her, Charlie. She must have wasted it all. Your hard-earned money down the drain. I guess you'll be crushing that car tomorrow. And then that better be the end of it. If she comes around looking for you at work again, I want you to let Richard and me know right away, alright?"

I nodded and continued watching the TV, but I wasn't thinking about *The Andy Griffith Show* anymore.

"I'm going to go take a bath, Charlie, and try to, I don't know, decompress."

I waited for her to shut the bathroom door, and then I zipped up my jacket and closed the front door behind me real quiet. I hoped I could catch Maria in time. I wanted to see her and tell her I was sorry and that I still wanted to be friends.

I walked the half mile to the salvage yard like always, past the snowbanks or what was left of them anyway.

When I got to the driveway, it was almost dark. I could just make out the yellow "Young's Salvage Yard" sign out front and the junk piles behind it. There was her car by the office, just like Nancy said, the gold 1951 Ford Crestliner.

As I got closer, I started hearing noises—like the desk moved and some things fell. Then I heard Maria say, "Oh, Richard." It was just like I always wanted her to say my name. She said it soft at first and then louder.

I knew what was happening in the office wasn't right and that I wasn't supposed to know about it. It was worse than when Maria said we couldn't be friends anymore. I started to think of all those times she came to the yard and Richard told me to keep working. Maybe I was stupid after all.

I didn't want to stay and listen, but I was frozen just like the snowbanks. Poor Nancy. I thought about talking to Richard, but then I could lose my job. After ten whole years. I already lost Maria. I couldn't lose my job too. I sat down in the gravel and leaned up against the building. Cracking my knuckles, I looked up at the sky.

A little while later after the noises stopped, I heard Maria say, "Richard, there's something important I need to tell you."

"Anything, Maria. What is it?"

"Well, it's hard to say. I didn't want this to happen. I know it's not what either of us expected."

"You can tell me, darling. What is it?" I never heard him call Nancy darling before.

"I'm pregnant, Richard."

*　　*　　*

Miller leaned back in his chair and crossed his arms. "Charlie, I'm going to be honest with you here—man to man, ok? This is Howland. We don't have murders here. We have good people, like you, just trying to make a living. The people need to know how this happened. They need to know who did this and why. I have a feeling you can help me tell them."

"I'm trying."

Miller looked frustrated. Then he and the other cop stood up.

"Alright, Charlie. Let's take a break. We're going to call Nancy in now."

I got up and followed them into the waiting room.

"Mrs. Young?" they asked.

I took her seat and tried not to think too much. It felt good to be out of that small room, but I couldn't sit still, kept thinking about what Nancy would find out in there.

*　　*　　*

After Maria told Richard, he didn't say anything right away. I think he was as surprised as me. He was lucky Ma wasn't around to see this. She'd have a cow. Worse than the day with the dog. Worse than the day Nancy told her *she* might be pregnant. She wasn't, which Ma said was a blessing.

"Well," Richard finally said. "We'll take care of it, that's all. We'll have to take care of it."

"Thank God," Maria sighed. "I can't do it alone. I know this is a lot for you. It's going to be messy, but maybe it'll be a good thing. It'll give us a real shot at this, Richard. It'll be a second chance for both of us."

"What are you talking about? I didn't mean we'll take care of the baby; I meant we'll take care of the pregnancy. I'll give you the money to go take care of it, and we'll keep it quiet, that's all."

"You can't be serious!"

"Of course I'm serious. What did you think was going to happen? That we'd send out an announcement?"

Maria's voice got real low. "I knew you were a cheater, Richard, but I didn't think you were a murderer."

"Just let me think. This is not what I needed right now!" Richard yelled.

"You think it's what I need? It's the last thing I need, Richard. I'm divorced, I'm working off tips at a diner, and now I'm pregnant with a baby I can't afford. You know Charlie's not giving me any more money, and now you're telling me you won't even help me with your own child? Nancy is just always going to get in the way, isn't she? You'll choose her and that inheritance every time. She's going to find out—one way or another, Richard."

My eyes started watering and my hands were sweating. I leaned over and put my head between my knees, trying to think.

I heard a slam. "Just let me think, Goddammit! You're a selfish woman, you know that? I should've known you'd pull something like this. I never thought I'd be as easy to con as Charlie, but I have to give it to you, Maria—you played us both."

"What are you saying? You think I planned this? You're out of your mind."

"What better way to keep me? That poor bastard, I really feel for him now."

I lifted my head from my knees. They were talking about me, about how Maria took advantage of me, just like Nancy said.

*   *   *

I was back at the yard at 9 a.m. for my shift like always. Richard shoulda been there already; he likes to go in early to look at numbers, he says. But that morning he told me he'd be late and that I should just go ahead and crush all the cars. He had a lot on his mind. I did too when I dropped the weight on the gold 1951 Ford Crestliner and watched the metal and glass cave in. I thought of Maria, of the baby, and felt sad.

#

"Thank you for your time, Mrs. Young. I know this isn't easy." Detective Miller shook Nancy's hand. "We'll let you know when you can see your husband next. Take care, alright? And let us know if you think of anything else that might be helpful—anything at all."

Nancy nodded and then looked at me. Her eyes were red. "Come on, Charlie," she said, grabbing my arm and walking to the door. The sun was setting, and Nancy's was one of the only cars in the parking lot.

"Charlie?" she asked, buckling her seatbelt. "Did you know about Maria—that she was pregnant?"

I looked down and cracked my knuckles. "No, I didn't know that."

Nancy wiped at her eyes. "Did you go to the yard that night while I was in the bath? Did you find out?"

"Find out what?" I put my hand into my pocket, feeling the cold metal of Maria's gold locket.

Nancy was quiet.

Ma always told us to protect each other. I think that's why Nancy kept looking at me even when I didn't look back and why she didn't say anything when she turned her eyes to the road, started the car, and headed for home.

Freedom   **(Crescent Beach)**
By Kim Rose

I was the creature whose shell lies
iridescent in the sand, on shimmering

sunlit constellations of speckled silt,
shifting under waves' persistent strokes

crushed glass, bone powder, fine
ground shark tooth, crab claw, ocean floor

litter: abandoned camouflage, every
ridge and groove proof – survival's a thin

disguise, like everything we put on
that gets chipped and worn over time

and time again. Now I wander the gravel edge
collecting fragments, each complete

my life's collection, husks like mine whisper
Braille under touch, the smooth language

of buried histories, how their fragile
armor glistens, as I systematically

discard the unbroken, leaving them for

others who like things easy

Selected Poems
By James Engelhardt

Practice

hours of rainy snow and my daughter
tries to make a snowman of the slush
which doesn't work

she comes in for cocoa
which I gladly make
and one for her mother, with a little bourbon

furnace rumbles, cars hiss past
the cats pad through, claws ticking on wood
Sunday is a day of quiet

a little nap time, a board game
but never enough,
even the snow is never enough

Rabbit

Each summer hotter than the last
and this afternoon a rabbit who

I imagine is the rabbit in the moon
has come to this shaded strip of grass

between the two low buildings
of my apartment complex.

She appears most days

finds a good patch of green and eats.

Whole dandelions disappear.
Today after feeding she stretches out

her rest almost domesticated—
forelegs up and back legs flat against earth.

She looks more content than I feel
hauling clothes to the laundry room.

Her ear twitches as she watches me.
We share the stillness of the air.

Birdwatching

The phoebe nesting on our porch dives
through the backyard, pulls up, hovers,
dives again and returns
to the abandoned satellite dish
then flashes back to the nest.

I tell the woman with the lotus tattoo
that love is like that
we fly out and return,
stars and magnetic fields guide us home.

But now cicadas pulse in the evening tension.
The return and return and return is the practice.
My wings fill with ink and smoke,
the house large enough to hold
the phoebes, cats, the small devotions
of living, and words as delicate as birdsong.

Sometimes I Go to the Cemetery
By Marian Willmott

Heavy, permanent, imposing,
wide as a headboard,
the polished granite guards
their bones,
lying below, side by side.

I lie down,
opening my heart
to feel a presence
but only a tall pine's quivering shadow,
brittle needles and reptile roots
embrace me.
They are not here.

My father is in his leather chair
lighting his pipe.
My mother is doing a crossword puzzle,
legs tucked under her.

Or she is rising,
dripping from the bath
while I watch with fascination
as she dries herself,
patting lilac powder
into her belly's fleshy folds,
under each heavy breast,
and between her thick thighs,
her body ripe, soft and sweet smelling.

The stone
only marks their time
blind
to the tendrils of their arms
entwining and blossoming.

A True Story
By Nina Smilow

You first overhear the story at a dinner your parents make you attend. You're young enough that it's whispered, like you don't know about the world yet. Like young people can't understand that kind of pain, even when the story is about a young person.

"They found his body in the East River and he was clinging on to this backpack," your father's friend said, "I mean, aren't you so fucking curious to know what's in that bag?"

The conversation moves on quickly from there because you are present. Someone asks you about how seventh grade is going. You think about your backpack, a Jansport, which most people in your class have. Its ubiquity makes you think that was the backpack they found with the boy. Yours is pink and corduroy and you think his probably wasn't. You decide in that moment that his was red. Years later, you'll think that maybe someone had mentioned it that night, but on days you try and research the event, you can't even find the story. It's lost in a sea of soaring bodies.

You answer that school is going fine.

After dinner in the car, you bring the story up. Your mother stays silent, but your father asks if it made you sad. The unspoken part of the conversation is that you've been crying at breakfast a lot lately. You lean forward and say that it's not so much that, you just think it's a crazy story. You think it would be a great movie or something. Your dad suggests you trademark the idea, which you didn't even know was an option for other people's stories.

It's a thrilling concept, that someone's tragedy can just be an idea you had for a piece of fiction. It gives you permission to hold on to the event and not be crushed under the weight of it. You decide he was around your age, barely a teenager which is, you think, almost an adult.

You fill in gaps: he went to school downtown and lived in Brooklyn. On nice days he walked across the Brooklyn Bridge instead of taking the subway home because he liked the view. He knew that bridge almost as well as the people who fell building it, maybe better because of his many successful journeys across. He owned it the way kids like you who are from New York own its public spaces, by inhabiting them more than any tourist could.

It was on one of these walks home that he became aware of the fact that he no longer cared about the view. He wasn't sure if he even felt capable of caring for anything anymore. He paused to look at the empty space of the towers that fell when he was too young to understand anything, but how scary it was. He only knew how much dust there was. How people jumped from windows-they were so scared.

That space didn't make him think of fear anymore and when they showed pictures to his class on the recent anniversary, he had just thought about how it looked more like flying than falling.

When the rest of his class sat at lunch after that memorial assembly and discussed the tragedy in terms that could be easily shared and understood by seventh graders, he didn't share his detachment. He was popular and knew better than to rock the boat. Instead, he concentrated on laughing when someone said something that was supposed to be funny, but every time he made an attempt to enjoy something, it took more effort than it did before. Like trying to claw out of quicksand.

Quicksand is so prevalent for kids, always appearing in cartoons or movies. It feels like it should come up more in life, but its real value is only ever metaphorical. Quicksand might be the most dangerous thing in adult life, since it seems like adults are often stuck and going down deeper in things that make them unhappy.

You imagine all of this during the car ride home. You create a person with these thoughts and then decide that he never shared them with his classmates or friends. They might have slipped out a few times at home or the guidance counselor's office, where he was sent when his grades started plummeting, where they were greeted with such confusion disguised as concern that he decided it was easier to improve his grades than try to explain it again. That's where he existed that day on the bridge. Maybe he thought he would just be woken up by climbing the railing.

Your imagination ends here because you can't make sense of the next literal step he takes or of why he had clung to the backpack so tightly that they found it still clutched in his hands despite the fall and the water. And sure, as you make the journey from the car to your bedroom, you grant that some of what you've put in his head borrows from your own thoughts after last weeks' 9/11 Memorial Assembly, but this fictional tragic hero is allowed to run much farther with them, because he is, after all, a story to be trademarked.

Obviously, you don't trademark the story, don't even investigate if that's really an option, because you're a middle schooler and the next day someone makes fun of your pants and that tragedy is all you can think about for the next few days. After you've gotten over that, your crush compliments a shirt and that victory owns the weekend.

That's part of being so young you're not aware of yet. No one is while it's happening. No one can understand how quickly their mind is traveling at that age and how deeply it can hold on to things for the briefest amount of time. Devastations that seemed insurmountable can be left behind moments later. Later you'll think about how important that knowledge would be to someone standing on the edge of a bridge, but this is not that moment. Right now, you're thinking about your crush.

*   *   *

The story comes back to you the summer before high school while you and your friends kill time in the way you do before killing time involves sneaking around to experiment with drugs, drinking, and sex. You get on the subway and end up where you end up and try and figure out what to do and then how to get home. This is how you discovered the hidden climbing tree in Prospect Park, the biggest and cheapest candy store in the Lower East Side, the diner from the 50's that still sells egg creams on the Upper East Side, the dangerous playground in Ft. Greene that never has kids in it, and the vintage store in Williamsburg where you buy your first crop top.

This time you've found yourself on the bridge from the story and you're looking around thinking how tricky it would be to find a way to jump. Then you're thinking about how often lately you've been looking for the edges of things—the subway platform, the street curb—and you remember the story you came up with on the drive home from a dinner you barely remember. You mention it to a friend walking with you, who laughs and says, "What the fuck was in the backpack?" Then the coolest kid in your class steals their hat and starts running and they chase after them. You never realized before, but you made a decision about that question.

He had drawings. You don't know why you think that. Probably because you know that if it had been something like a weapon, or jewelry, or even money, that would have been part of the synopsis of the event and made it less tragic, more criminal. You assume that if there had been a computer or cellphone, they would have retrieved what was on it. It must have been paper, but you can't imagine leaping off a bridge for the sake of any homework you've ever done. It leaves you with the sense of a notebook. Maybe because you have one filled with what might someday be stories, but you want to keep creating distance between you and your subject so that you can keep thinking about him. So, it's an art, but one that you never attempt.

He had drawn someone he was romantically interested in. He loved them so much, because you know that love is something very powerful that you want and that terrifies you. You actually think you might even be on the brink of it and the whole thing is so overwhelming that you feel your feet are barely on this bridge's raised ground.

You decide it must have been unrequited or dangerous in some way, since right now the text messages you're getting feel like they're lifting you out of quicksand and your notebook has taken a turn from the morbid to the saccharine, so if his was a loss, it must have been one that was total. The obvious answer is that the object of his affection was dead, but you just started understanding love; that kind of loss is still hazy on the horizon of your comprehension.

You remember the kinship you felt at that dinner, when you were introduced to the story of this boy. Now you've tied another line, because in class last year when someone spoke about the stupidity of Romeo and Juliet's joint suicide, you thought there could be nothing else important enough to die for.

So, you can understand if he drew pictures of this person and that's what was in the backpack. For some reason, they wouldn't ever be with him and that, on top of the deep isolating pain you established for him when you first heard the story, sent him plummeting. Here you've gained both perspective and distance from the narrative and him. You can understand it, but not perceive yourself as under the same threat. Because you can acknowledge that some aspect of this constant crafting of the story comes from your fear of your comprehending it. When the question passed over the dinner table, it was with a distant curiosity for the adults, but it hung for you like a math question you would be tested on later. If you studied hard enough, a right answer would reveal itself to you.

That's part of this moment in life. Where every answer produces new questions. Your first kiss only leads to more firsts, each one feeling bigger than the last. Your world is made up of things to experience so you can't see beyond the experiences yet.

You used to be worried about not feeling enough and now you're becoming a creature of heightened senses. Hunger has become starvation, being tired is now exhaustion, attraction has become all encompassing, and curiosity has become a burning urge to fly.

*   *   *

Now you're almost done with high school. The boy's story stopped being a narrative shortly after you aged past him. It's become part of the series of poems in the back of your school notebooks. Now he's never the popular boy you imagined him to be when you were in middle school. Nor is he unpopular. He's an outcast in these new spaces. Someone who doesn't fit in any definable genre given to young people by other young people. He was very, very lonely, you think, and try to create a space for the loneliness.

This is partly because the peak of puberty brought popularity into your life and it made you understand loneliness like you never had before. Then it showed you that if you created him as popular, no one would believe in his isolation.

It reminds you of last weekend at a party when everyone agreed to discuss their anxieties about their upcoming collegiate departures. At first you had felt so relieved to know that it wasn't just you who saw graduation as less of a celebration and more like being asked to land safely after being pushed off a mountain.

Quickly though, you were undone when people voiced concerns over future roommates and possibly inadequate laundry situations. Your anxiety was not so pragmatic. Were you supposed to suddenly achieve happiness just because you left high school? What would it mean if you didn't and never did? These fears stayed pursed on your lips and you did a shot of whiskey that burned from your mouth to your toes and turned your fears to ashy thoughts.

Somehow this self-imposed silence leads you to be certain that he didn't jump with the backpack anymore, but after it. Someone threw it over the edge. Other boys from his school, possibly, maybe a crazy stranger, like the man in twelve coats on the hottest day of last July who told you he was going to fuck your skull, which was so insane you laughed until he started chasing you.

The boy jumped to get the bag. The fact that catching a bag while plummeting is likely impossible changes nothing about your certainty. He jumped for the bag. The fall was secondary to the act of catching it, though the result wasn't unknown to him when he took the leap. But at least this way he wasn't just chasing an ending, he was also seeking something, and it was in the bag. It was all about the backpack, your poems have decided.

The really absurd thing is that you still think it had drawings. Now you believe that in his outcast status he fell in love with someone who would never be with him. The potential loss of the images of this unattainable person as he saw them was the last thing he could bear.

Because you're still young, as everyone keeps telling you, but you're older than they think you are because you know there are things that people can't take. You know about losses and sufferings that you cannot endure, learned early in high school, where that first love aged you. It was filled with lessons you would never want anyone to have to learn. Like what it is to want to get away from something in your own head so badly that you create distance between yourself and the world.

That bridge you keep putting between yourself and your story has become smaller in the last four years. Maybe that's why it can't just be a story anymore even in a poem. It's a series of questions sinking into the answers you think you found, ones that terrify you.

Answers that point to the fear that what was dismissed as childish angst is formalizing itself. Your mind is cementing pathways and ideas. This story is becoming a part of the same hard wiring that drags you down the same routes and routines every day. You're being increasingly concreted and where you thought you would detach from the story, that it might become something to be shared casually again, it's become structural.

*   *   *

You go to college still in your city and take a screenwriting class. When you talk about what to compose at dinner, your father reminds you of the story. The memory of the possible boy and backpack doesn't alarm you as much as the fact that anyone else remembers them. It's almost like you forgot that this was once part of a collective curiosity, since it's belonged to you for so long now. You nod and smile and say, "Maybe" and you mean it. For the next few days, you sit in the library and try to craft an outline.

An outsider and their pain, unrequited love and everything it involves, that's the story you have. However, you're older again and you see new gaps. You see where you'll never get an audience to sympathize, because they'll be older too and as you get older, it gets harder to imagine jumping for drawings. Yet, some part of you is attached to the idea, the part that people are still calling so young. You can't edit it enough, can't get rid of the idea of an illogical reach for something. He was, you think determinedly, jumping for something. That thing must have been in that bag.

The story has popped in your head every time you see a Jansport. It's made you want to go to every owner of the bag and ask to explore the contents. You know you're looking for a reason outside of the obvious one. You're looking for a new logic behind why someone takes flight with inevitable failure. You want to think it's what's in a bag, but now you're realizing that what's embarrassing about that dinner is how much everyone didn't realize that the bag had nothing to do with it. No one jumps for a bag. They jump when there's nothing else.

All the stories you've come up with for him; his sexual and romantic desires, his mental or physical illnesses, his family trials, all these things you gave voice to in your head every time you thought about the boy, they're all circling around the swift movement between standing and falling that enticed you at a meal years ago. That's what you realize in the library. You weren't horrified or saddened at the story. You were just curious.

You wanted to know if the backpack held a secret key to the next step, because you always understood something that the adults weren't supposed to have missed. You knew, without knowing you had the information, why someone would jump without a secret backpack and you didn't want that to be it for this boy. You wanted him to have had a better reason than because he wanted to fall.

You close your computer and leave because there's nothing else you can do. You meet your friends at a bar. Everyone bitches about the school's elective policy and trying to find apartments to rent and you laugh and nod and feel the structure of your imagination collapsing. Someone you used to date who you think wishes you were still dating mentions the screenwriting class and asks what you're working on. You say truthfully that you don't know and before anyone can question what you were doing in all that time at the library, you ask a girl in the drama program about her show and let her take the conversation away.

You know that the people around you would listen to your conundrum and hear writer's block. You know they would guide you forward, but you also know this isn't a story anymore. You can't craft it, trademark it, or shift it to be something different. It's just a tragedy now and you just want to stop it from ever having happened. You want to take away all the reasons for it, but those reasons are life.

*   *   *

Time has done what it does, when you don't interrupt it, and grown you up. You've gone from being almost a teenager to almost an adult to being called an adult constantly, though you've stopped waiting to feel like one. You're done with graduations and classmates and off to put what you learned into practice in the real world. You're at the age where you're supposed to understand pain.

You know something now that will prevent you ever from writing the story, even if you constantly search all the engines for the answer. You know that the answer lies in not finding one and maybe that is being an adult.

You remember being young and not knowing you'd ever know more. You remember how it seemed like there was a finite number of moments that would define you. You couldn't know how capable humans are of change when so much of the change in your life had been unconscious. Your body stretched, your voice deepened, and you wanted to touch people in places you never thought of. You watched decisions get made for you and about you, which meant you made most of your own choices based on defiance. You had felt so stuck in all these decisions and thought they were the root of all the understanding you had for the boy. You didn't imagine you'd one day possess some control, which would be more terrifying than the absence of it, but also make you stronger. You couldn't know that every time you endured something terrible, it would make you better at the next thing to come.

You're standing on that bridge again, this time by yourself, walking home after work, and it seems like a series of lives have passed since you stood there to kill time and especially since you heard the story. You've fallen in love and out of it and in it again and then again. You've been to funerals and weddings. You pay your own bills and have dinner parties with your own friends where someone always brings up something they've read about in the news.

You've tried by now to write about the boy, to research his story, to understand it, and it's never worked. If it's even true and the event took place, it was never a story and definitely not yours to tell. It was only a young person who already knew what it's taken you so long to learn.

It was about a jump, which is about everything that leads to an edge. You only know the things someone can know when they get to the other side of the bridge. When you've fought the doomed impulse of flight for long enough. Here's the truth: you understood a child who committed suicide when you were a child who wanted to. Maybe you were the same, except he jumped. You didn't. You keep walking. It's enough.

Picking Violets Before the Apocalypse
By Catheryne Gagnon

What I know is,
the world didn't always look this way –
it had a different shape,
I remember it soft, curved like the lines in a palm,
and quiet as the air just after a storm,
release hanging between the strands of static.

We're all dying, just very slowly,
so slow it feels like stillness,
so slow I don't feel it at all.
What I feel is the sky
melting into a shimmering pool
of pavement,
the heat like a film on my skin,
your heartbeat ringing in
the tips of my fingers.

I catch a glimpse of tenderness
but it recedes into the veins of the leaves.
If all that's left at the end of it all
are remnants, wandering ghosts,
I think mine will curl up in the hearts of
woodlands the wildfires spared,
pouring salve on everything that burned.

Now I stand on the tips of my toes
watching the sun slide over the water,
the light cutting through in an uneven line.
When it's all gone, will we deserve
the absolution of a clean cut?
We were just a flicker
before we poured the gasoline.

The stars sink into a tendril of ocean
with a sigh, barely a ripple, but it is
the riptide I am waiting for.
The taste of metal lingers on my tongue
maybe I sliced my lip
on the trail of stubble along your throat
or the hard edge of the world.

Selected Poems
By Camille Lebel

Things I Can't Answer for my Disabled Son

Whether or not flamingos dream.
Why we speak of yesterday but refuse the yesternight.
If a tree can grow as high as the clouds and
why humans cannot shed their skin all at once,
like a snake.

And should he believe in God?

In vacation Bible school,
a hallway becomes the belly of a whale.
Devoted teachers show the way,
send the little children through
into the darkening depths.
Tiny, faithless Jonahs
delivered to sanctuary, meat
for the bare-ribbed pews.

The faithful school my son in praises
to a good Father, the all-powerful creator
who holds the world in his hands
but left this boy's legs twisted, muscles stretched tight.
Is the omniscient eye so charmed by the sparrow
that He lost sight of this one small boy?

With wide-mouthed puppets,
devoted voices sing of grace,
preach of bodies formed in perfect likeness,

stand together on the promises while
my son sits silent on the front row.

We deliver him to surgeons.
Scalpels sharp, they reshape his creation,
wiring wayward limbs into form with titanium.
We fit still-growing legs into hard, plastic molds,
correcting posture, gait, balance.
His divine image requires transformation.

Slinging unceasing questions into the cosmos,
he wants to know if
velociraptors occupied the ark if
heaven will have video games if
mortal feet can walk upon water
why
must he fall
walking across the room?

I tell him no more questions for today.

The Living Room Rug

The daughter refuses floor coverings

In her childhood home,
a rug lies heavy on the
wooden floor,
a sensible mid-grade replica
thick and durable

synthetic
respectable

A lotus blossom border lies
enlightenment
rooted in filth

Stories trapped beneath
lurk under careful feet,
fingernail shards, ripped from the quick
gin-sick stains disguised
sweetly burning on the round trip journey
intricate textile diamonds covering
claw marks
spilled blood, faded to wine

On rainy days, the stench slides through;
a damp, rotting creature writhing up
between the threaded fringe,
winding around ankles,
paralyzing tongues

But she will not be muffled this day,
she demands the truth of a sharp-striking
heel upon hardwood,
her feet resist sinking into the centered medallion

Aching fingers find the corner
peeling back the weight,
a bandage removed from wound, stinging
new skin demands air

Jaw clenched firm, molars grinding
she rolls decaying bodies
into fibers of cream, gold, burgundy;
dragging the rug to the backyard
she sets it ablaze

Threads untangle, curling into smoke
freed from constraint of design
blossoms burst into light

Inside, Mother beholds the remnants of
life, uncovered
buckled boards, breaking where they
could not expand
peeling layers of precisely-applied finish
rippled wear from marching to the drum's
relentless beat.

A practiced finger traces words
carved by silence

Mother makes her plan to buy a new rug

When the Hero Has Cerebral Palsy

His body never
poetry. Feet slap-scooting,
too flat on the floor.

Twisted legs not quite
finding the gaited couplet--
aching dissonance.

Limbs of other boys
rhythmically schemed in stanzas
strong and well-behaved.

For kicking the ball,
running the race, standing to pee--
like a man.

Graceful fingers, long,
too fragile to tie his pants
scratch his rage on skin.

Longings: stomp away,
slam a door, throw a chair, more--
Carry his own plate.

But two steps into
running away, the line breaks,
a cursed caesura.

Head hitting the wall
sharp elbows askew, finding
unyielding concrete.

Unstressed, stressed, repeat.
No combination allows
musicality.

His mother comes near,
a tired refrain: loving lies;
he shoves her away.

Fingers grip counter
Superhuman, rising up
again and again

He questions God who
cages him; spasticity,
Grendel's best weapon.

This is his epic;
a pilgrimage, here to there.
The dragon inside.

Under the Sun
By A.J. Granger

We are all raisins—

waiting on the bus to hell,

out of juice—thirsty,

uncertain when we fell.

Earth
By Vanessa Garcia

The first time I met her I said: "Hey, Sidewalk Sue, why you got a piece of paper up your nostril, huh?"

"So my soul don't go," she said.

"Shit," I said, "that's heavy."

That was before I knew how to talk to them, before I saw what a Humvee rolling over an IEV could do to a person's head – cracked skull or not, it jumbled everything; memories got shifted and light didn't filter the same through eye sockets, and it wasn't always because of banged up retinas. I mean, hell, I didn't even really know what IEV meant before. Now I do: Improvised Explosive Device. Bad words in the desert are always abbreviated.

Now I look at Sue and I wish I could make her a waterproof tent.

She's always the first one outside when we open, standing on the sidewalk there, every morning before 8:15 for god knows how long before I get to work, with tissues up both her nostrils, like little rockets she's made to stopper the river of red.

"Sometimes they bleed," she says this morning, pointing to her nose-holes.

"I know," I tell her. I've seen it. Way it all pours from her face like when you get a tooth boxed out of you.

"Did it bleed this morning?" I ask her.

"Yeah."

I can see there are still traces of maroon on the tissues. I fiddle with the lock on the roll-up aluminum door. Every morning I wonder about this thing – why there isn't some high-tech alarm instead of a lock and a roll-up aluminum door. "Can't the government get us a new damn lock?" I mumble out loud.

"No, they're building more MRAPs," says Sue, "it's better that way. Wish I'd been in one of those instead of a shit Humvee."

MRAP: Mine-resistant, ambush-protected vehicles.

Sue's boyfriend left her when she came back the last time. I mean, hell, I get it, I've gotten left for less reasons. And wouldn't I do the same thing, if I were him – take care of a dribbling, drooling, idiot all your life? It's a serious question. But she wasn't like that anymore. She was like that right off the bat at Walter Reade, she told me once, but she's better now. Walter Reade was like Fantasy Land, she said.

"It's not like the real world, you know, everybody gets it over there, they take care of you, and there aren't any water and phone bills to pay, you know what I'm saying?"

I wonder what she was like before.

I finally get the rusty lock open, and roll up the door, wiping off the red residue from the lock on my jeans. Sue follows behind me. "You see Sira today, right?" I ask.

"Yeah," she sighs. But then there's the edge of a smile at the corner of that sigh. Because Sira can do that to you.

The best days are the days Sira comes in. She makes this place; has gotten so popular with the vets that they don't go to the VA anymore, they come here – at least for the post-traumatic stress stuff, not for the physical injuries, we're not equipped for that. We don't have that much grant money, so she struggles all the time to keep us open, and the other shrinks aren't all that great, so it's just her carrying the load. But she's used to it. She has a shaved head and a big chunky watch that makes her look like she's prepping to go scuba diving or something. "It keeps good time," Sira says, deadpan, when I make fun of her. She's skinny like little boys are skinny and she doesn't have any boobs and her nails are bit sometimes to where you see little nubby bumps of skin protruding from under her nail. But she's so, I don't know...feline, no matter what she does to hide it, it's like she's this scarf blowing in the wind when she walks through the door. I wish I looked like her. I'm one of those girls that looks like a little boy because I'm so small, not because I try to, but because I got a comfy pixie cut and don't wear any make up and that sort of thing. I probably look more like a little boy that looks like a girl than a girl that looks like a boy, like David Bowie or something (yeah right, I wish). It's complicated, obviously. Anyway, one day Sira came to work in this psychedelic Sari and I wondered what the hell a half Iranian chick was doing in an Indian dress. Her stomach showed through it, like brown sugar and that was the first time I thought to myself: Shoot, Sira's the coolest person I know...Until I met Sue. Now they're tied.

Sue waits at the counter for the sign-up sheet while I switch on all the lights.

"Sira's pretty good to you?" I say handing over the sign-up. I bet if we looked up all the sign-up sheets, Sue would be the first one on the list every day. I can't vouch for my days off, but I'd bet.

"Sira's great," she says, capping the pen.

"You making progress then?"

"Yeah, although, you know, sometimes I want to remember what I can't and I don't want to remember what I can. It's a problem," she says, starting to walk away towards one of our orange, plastic chairs ready to stick her head in a book while she waits for Sira to get in. Sue's been reading Classics lately, I don't know what she finds in them but sometimes she's got her face so close to the book it looks like the book's going to eat her, like those man-eating plants, and like her little body (she's only a little taller than me) is going to be sticking out from the bottom of this book-plant, and she'll try to see but she won't be able to because she's got pages for a face.

Sira's brother is dead. She's lived on the civilian side of battle. That's why she's so good at it now, at knowing what to say to the soldiers. War doctor.

"How'd you live with it when you were over there," I asked Sira once, "like, knowing something's gonna be blown up by some psycho on a mission anytime, anywhere, anyhow, with some improvised bullshit or some high-power nuclear cap-sized bomb up your ass."

"You get used to it," she said. "The worst is the aftermath."

She knew how to clean things up good. She was usually just straight to the point when she talked, but sometimes she let herself get carried away, and I kind of like it when she did that. Like when it was just the two of us in the back room, drinking day-old coffee, sometimes she said things I got stuck in.

"These people. They've lost touch, so many of them. They forget the meaning of things. Like hearth, they don't know what that means anymore. Take out the h, and that's all we really have, isn't it? Just a plot of land, whatever ground, some dirt, water, grass if you're lucky."

"It's not all bad, girl," I told her.

"No."

I looked up "hearth" when I got home. And for days I kept wishing I had a fireplace I could sit in front of.

Sue walks into Sira's office in her baggy jeans. Pulling her right leg a little, only slightly. You wouldn't be able to tell anymore, unless you knew. I imagine those jeans fit her once. Her body looks like it's been carrying something heavy for a really long time, like she's permanently in a sloshed-up rain coat. I wish I knew Sue more; wish I could touch her somewhere other people hadn't.

By the time the dust settles at work and everybody's in their place for the day, there's a period of waiting (waiting for the next sign-in; waiting for Sue to come out so I can say goodbye; waiting for Sira to come out of the office after her first few patients, so I can ask her the time. I love it when she looks at her big mamma watch). I fill the waiting with news, things that are supposed to be new but they're not.

All the newspapers talk about these days is the bailout plan and the financial crisis. Wall Street's got us in a bind; Washington can't get us out. I read that Wall Street's called Wall Street because way before, when the Dutch were in New York, they built a big wall to keep the Brits out. And then when the wall got torn down all that remained was the road that'd stood beside the wall: Wall Street. Everything's about war. Every time Pat comes back, he says that being back home is like being dead, and that life is really over there. War is life and life is death. "Now that's fucked up," I told him. I remember playing GI Joes when we were kids and Pat was always protecting the soldiers, putting them under the bed and in corners so I wouldn't find them with my missiles and take their heads off. I was the only girl in my class that preferred knocking down Joes to having Ken make-out with Barbie. It was probably because of Pat, because I would rather be with him, rile him up, impress him with my aim. It was better than twiddling my thumbs or braiding some blonde doll's hair. Now Pat takes pictures of the Joes for newspapers, but I hardly ever see them. He says it's because I don't read the right papers. Says it's important to record. *"War is a force that gives us meaning*; it's a book, you should read it," he told me. Supposedly that was supposed to make me "get it" better. I ordered it from Amazon a week ago, before he left again. Hasn't gotten here yet.

The classifieds used to be comforting when I'd had enough of the front page and the world section and even the sports section. Like that there were so many jobs people could take, that there were so many houses that people could buy and sell and live in; everything was rolling. But now everything's a Foreclosure. How depressing is that? Sometimes I think: I should buy a house. I mean, hell, I'm not rich, but I've been saving 10% of my income since I was a twelve-year-old snot selling hot dogs with dad. Why not make a little investment – buy low; sell high. Roger says this is the worst time to be coming home: "If regular people are in trouble, imagine what these guys feel like." Roger should know, he's been working here since Nam.

What does that really mean anyway – coming home? The place that's most home is just so long ago that I don't think I could ever get there again, no matter how hard I tried. Mom's kitchen, the floor she laid out herself. Tiles, orange, "imported from Spain, my little ones, from Spain," she liked to say, smiling ear to ear, mom in her red dresses, who could smile and light up a room. The window over-looking the terrace, and the fire-red bougainvillea that bloomed every year so that the leaves filled the pool like blood drops. "Damn this tree," dad said every Spring, net in hand every day. The bathroom where I stepped on a nail that dad took out with his hands before he took me to the hospital for a Tetanus Shot. "Big girls don't cry," he said. And I didn't. Pat's room, where he'd hidden stashes of weed from mom and dad, and where he'd had his Rasta phase and fallen in love with Bob Marley and a girl named Huckleberry. "One Love," he'd call out every time he said goodbye. "Loser," I'd call back. I miss him. I wonder what Palestine is like. We lived like kings and queens.

When Sue comes out of Sira's office, she always makes a ruckus. It's always out she goes with a big bad bang of the door. I can't tell if she doesn't notice she does it, or if she just doesn't care. Boom. And then right toward me to sign-out.

"Sira just told me I should make some friends," Sue says.

"You should."

"Want to come to my house tomorrow night? Maybe have dinner or something?"

It was kind of weird, her saying that so out of the blue, but I always wondered what Sue did when she wasn't around this place. Some of the other vets had kids or grandkids who they showed you pictures of and some of them had jobs, and some of them went back to school and were learning all kinds of things like how to become nurses or getting their MBA's, and some of them had picked up the piano, and one of them even started dancing Flamenco, which was really pretty bizarre I thought until I saw her dance one day and I said: wow, girl, why'd you go to war when you can shake and bake like that?

But that wasn't Sue. Sue was a mutt, sometimes she looked like a bum and sometimes she looked like a flower. I wondered about the handbook, if it was "conflict of interest" going to her house.

"So? You wanna come to my house or what?"

"Um, yeah, sure, I guess. Why not?"

"Okay."

Even if it was "conflict of interest," it was better to get fired than say no. After all, it'd been a direct command from Sira to Sue: socialize.

Sue's house was super neat and super clean. The furniture looked like it had been vacuumed twice daily since she'd bought it and the Persian-looking rug in the middle of the floor had the end threads spread out perfect like she'd gotten down on all fours and spread the tassels out with a toothpick.

"Spoils of war," said Sue when she saw me looking at the rug.

"What do you mean?"

"It was from a house in Baghdad, their grandfather had made it by hand. They thought I saved their lives so they gave it to me. Didn't make sense, carrying it around, so I said I'd be back for it when my time was done and I did, I went back to their house and brought it home, even though it was dangerous as shit to go back there."

"They thought you saved their lives? Did you?"

"That depends what you wanna call life. I shot a guy who was going to run crazy into their village and blow the whole thing up. Shot him up close, his yellow guts splattered all over my face. People think there isn't one-on-one combat like that anymore. But that's not true."

"How'd you know what he was going to do?"

"It was just part of one of our missions, we had information."

"Wow."

"No, not really."

On the wall closest to the rug, there was a bookshelf which looked like a theatre set or painting or something because the books were all lined up so straight. I wanted to look closer at it but Sue kept walking fast through the living room so I followed her. We walked through to the kitchen, where everything was even cleaner. A cockroach's nightmare, nowhere to hide. The towels hanging from the stove looked like they were dry-cleaned and had tiny hummingbirds sewn on them by hand, and everything in the whole house smelled like baby powder on a sleeping baby, like when you put your nose to the creases of one and it's like heaven. I walked over to the towels with the hummingbirds and wondered if Sue'd made them, was about to ask, when —

"—I don't really live here," she said.

When I asked her what she meant, she said she lived downstairs, in the den. When she got nervous, she came up here and she organized things and she cleaned; she liked the feeling of making everything perfect.

That wasn't really an explanation, but I didn't want to push her right away because all of a sudden she looked like she might break again.

Eventually I followed her down a set of steps into a much darker room than the rest of the house. No windows and it didn't smell like baby anymore. It smelled like wet rock. You might think a place that smells like wet rock would feel stone-cold too, but it didn't, it was kind of warm and cozy despite the smell. It was just as neat as on top but a little more lived in. Like there were footprints in the carpet, memories of her steps from this afternoon.

The whole thing was a little old-school with old wood paneling and there were books down here too, and although they were neat, they weren't as crazy-neat as the ones upstairs. There was a stack of about ten of them on a coffee table. A lot of them were the classical stuff I'd seen her reading at work. *The Bacchae, Medea, The Trojan Women, Lysistrata,* etc. And then books like, *Tell me How this Ends: General David Petraeus and the Search for a Way Out of Iraq.* There was brown, really short-haired carpeting from the seventies laid out everywhere, wall to wall. It had orange and reddish paisley print smeared all over it. It was a little tacky but it was ok.

There was a fridge and a small kitchenette, and she had similar white towels down here too, but these didn't have hummingbirds sewn on, they were tree-women instead. Women that had tree branches for heads and leaves for fingers. Really weird-looking, but kind of beautiful. On one of the chairs of the kitchenette there was a basket full of sewing supplies which answered my question about her making the hummingbirds and those tree-women. But the weirdest thing of all was that there were canned foods all lined up along the walls, like fortressing or something or like soundproofing in a studio.

"This is where I live," she said.

I didn't get it, I told her. Why did she do this and, more importantly, had she told Sira because this was something she should definitely tell Sira. She said she did tell Sira and when I asked her what Sira said, Sue said: "Nothing. Not yet, anyway. I'm sure she'll have something to say eventually but usually she lets me try and figure things out for myself first." As Sue said this, she walked toward the fridge and got us two beers.

"So, what's the point then of going to her? Couldn't you just sit here and think?"

"No, not really. My mind gets neater when I talk to Sira. Like when I bake bread. That happens too. Clean, and neat, and quiet. There's something about Sira that makes it happen, the way she nudges little by little, kinds of questions she asks. Questions you just don't ask yourself but which you have to face if you're sitting in front of her and have nowhere to go, and want to get better. I don't know what it is and I can't place my finger on it, but she just makes everything neater," she said. "Cheers."

The necks of or bottles touch.

"And you like things neat," I say, winking, going to sit on her love-seat.

She knows I'm pulling her leg so she laughs and she comes to sit next to me. I'd never seen her laugh before. Her cupid-bow mouth opening up to the whitest, straightest teeth. I'd also never seen her eyes so close-up before, how green they were, like muted camouflage.

"Sometimes when I look over at the bed, I have these visions and they scare me."

"Like what?" I ask, trying to catch what's there, hiding behind the green of her eyes.

"I see myself there, and there are all these men and women grabbing at my arms and legs and chewing on them and I can't escape. It's like a harem of cannibals and the blood starts to stain everything and it all turns red, and sometimes I faint and I wake up on the floor."

I want to kiss her when she says this. It's a strange violent feeling, like I had with the GI Joes when I was a kid, like I want to shoot her with an arrow and then catch her and breathe life into her. And then that violence meets a feeling like a magnetic pull between us which has been there before but which I'd always tried to ignore. It's just like that, like when you have two magnets facing each other and the force of it keeps making them closer even though you're trying really hard to keep them apart. I wish I could see that space between the magnets, see what it's made up of, maybe I'd understand everything a little better, maybe I could hear Pat better when he talks to me from so far away, maybe I can learn to be there for him when he comes back, maybe I can be here for Sue. But I don't know what that means, so I ask more questions.

"Do you see the same thing in the upstairs bed?" I ask her.

"No. Upstairs it's worse because I can't remember."

"What can't you remember?"

"There's this whole part of my life, right before I got deployed the last time, right around the time that we bought the house, that I can't remember. It's like I can't remember what it's like to live up there and what's the point of being up there if it's not somewhere in your memory?"

"So, you decided to move down here?"

"When Tim left, I picked up some of my stuff and came down here. He left me the house because he felt guilty and I hated that, but I didn't have anywhere to go, not even the house really. I don't even know if that makes sense. Anyway, little by little, I brought more and more things down here and started making a new home without knowing it; new history."

"Jesus, Sue."

"What?"

"I don't know. It just makes me sad."

"Why?"

"I don't know," I say.

And then we're both quiet for a while and Sue takes off her shoes. Her toe nails are painted red, which is such a surprise, red like mom's dresses.

"What's with the cans?" I ask her, still staring at her toes, sort of nervously, not knowing what to else to say, and also out of a genuine curiosity.

"For just in case," she says shrugging her shoulders.

"Just in case what?"

"You know…"

"The end?" I say, sort of making fun of her.

"Yeah. But it's not really all that funny."

There was another little quiet moment while I thought about it. And I guess it wasn't funny. How scared she must be and how it wasn't really about the end of the world, but about watching friends lose limbs and noses and eyes. And watching herself fall into a long trap of time, dragging her leg, stepping into rooms where there were parts of herself missing; a seizured past shaken from her. And here she is, picking up her red-toes, bringing them to her hips, sitting Indian style next to me, looking like her head is heavy and she wants somewhere to lean on.

"That would be a shame, wouldn't it?" I tell her.

"What?" she asks, looking up at me.

"If it all disappeared. If it all went to shit." If you weren't sitting here next to me, or me to you. "If all the houses fell to the ground around us, and we all sort of went up in dust."

And then Sue takes her hand and puts it in mine, and I feel like I used to feel with Pat, like she has me, like she's protecting me and I feel so strange inside, happy and sad at the same time, and full of this bumping thing running all over through my inside channels, like I should be protecting *her*, but here she is, holding *my* hand. I get a sharp little pang by my heart, everywhere warnings that I might rip open if I let it happen -- explode. And then she starts dripping, a little stream coming from her nose. She lifts her hand to stop it, but before her hand gets to her face, my tongue is already there, seeping up the blood. Because maybe I could take it in, keep it inside me, and give it back to her, clean, breath her blood back into her mouth like a dialysis machine clearing up her soul. Maybe this is what Sira meant, about the things we've got: sitting here with Sue, on this tiny plot of earth, nobody's home but our temporary shelter.

Selected Poems
By Karen McAferty Morris

At the Thrift Store

On the shelf beside Candyland, Pictionary, and Sorry
a helter-skelter array of jigsaw puzzle boxes
add their faded rainbow hues to the other
worn-cornered cast-off items of entertainment--
kittens, a snowy New England farm, tulip fields and a windmill,
and Disney princesses, ranging from fifty to one thousand pieces.
I hadn't done a jigsaw puzzle in years, but link them to family
Myrtle Beach vacations, maybe something to spend
a few minutes a day doing, now that there is more time to fill.

Her small, disheveled figure sidles close,
wrinkles score her thin cheeks, her short gray hair sprouts
from a woolen cloche tilted like a pan lid toward one ear
above bald patches, her coat collar is stained.
I want to edge slowly away.

"That one looks nice," she gestures to the puzzle box I am holding.
I agree. "With those different colored flowers, maybe
it wouldn't be too hard to fit them all together,
not like those where all the pieces look exactly the same."
I return it to the shelf. She holds out a pocketbook
with a $4 tag attached, opens it wide. "I didn't put these in,"
she says. Inside rest a little round mirror, a red vinyl
change purse with a snap clasp, a pen with a purple feather on top.
"I wouldn't do that," she says meekly as if I thought
she was trying to steal them. Her fingers are so twisted
that I can't see how she can hold a fork, a toothbrush, a comb,
button a blouse, crack an egg, write her name.

I want to ask, "Do you have someone here with you? Who

helps take care of you? What kind of life do you have?"
I should make conversation, ask her which games
she played when she was young, does she have grandchildren.

But I am unnerved by her nearness, the safe distance we're all
used to keeping these days. I suppose that's why.
I mumble goodbye and wheel my cart to the kitchen
section where I look for a glass bowl big enough for salad,
popcorn, or potatoes, something not too breakable.

Burned Down

I happened to drive by today, and saw it again
just around the corner from my house, burned down
three years ago, unkempt and rundown before that,
home of a down-and-out Navy veteran, then plumber
for a while, so I heard, and casualty of drink, at the end
rating visits from social workers and community nurses,
one notable time wheeling himself around the neighborhood
in nothing but a hospital gown asking for a can of beer.

The house caught fire one night, who knows how,
passed out maybe, a cigarette slipped from limp fingers,
blazed up fast, though he made it out to sprawl
in the road, carted off to a VA hospital after that.

For the longest time his scorched old Toyota sat in
the heaved-up driveway, the back of the house black
and gaping, the brick fireplace not looking all that
out of place, no stranger to fire, purpose-built.

Surviving the awful heat, orange trees and crepe myrtle,
pine trees and oak still cloistered it, then finally everything
manmade was razed, claimed, I saw today, by waist-high weeds

and sprightly, tall wild white daisies. I heard he died
not long after, asleep forever now under a white cross.

I wonder what I would have done if I'd been home
when you rolled yourself up my sidewalk that summer day,
thirsty, hot, desperate, would I have given you
a cold one, we could have talked some on the porch,
what'd you do in the service, can I make you a sandwich,
how'd you fall so low, do you have a dog?

Dock Lights

It is only May but the dock and high water around it,
and I, are being suffocated by the sweltering noon sun.
I have checked the banks for sunning turtles,
the pilings for any clinging crabs, have seen
the ripples of the mullet in their looping search for food.

Now I walk back across the green yard shadowed
and the dying myrtle tree whose leaning branches
I love, and for some reason remember when your husband
draped tiny white lights along the dock for my wedding.

Some years ago now, in a clear, blue, brisk November
afternoon we all stood there for the ceremony. Then as
day darkened, those lights glimmered like candles
on an altar, a place to watch for those returning from sea.

Last year at the Athens airport, I saw him turn
around and around between the luggage carousels,
confused, till you took his hand. Small things betraying.
You ordered his meals, helped him finish sentences,
when you looked at him, your smile a benediction.
Ancient people worshipped in soaring-columned temples,
broken by time, but we four were in awe and happy.

And you go on. You continue to take your trips,
plan pilgrimages to beautiful places where you both
take photographs, lugging your cameras and tripods,
laboring to find the dramatic angles, the perfect light

Joy is the Scariest Emotion
By Abigail Leigh

Sorrow is a familiar friend
Someone to rub up against
Grooved wound finger-traced over again
Linens wrinkled from over wear
In its wake, something to hold or mend, as coin or cloth
A concept conceivable
A home, recognizable
In the winter, at least, you expect to be cold

But joy is a strange wind
Blowing across your doorstep
A scent of peaches perfumed
Songs rippling from the stereo
Requires nothing
What do you do with something that floats?
No pieces to pick up, no threads to sew, no way to contain—
Arrival unannounced
It drifts just as easily away

Joy threatens the comfortable dark
With its intangible touch
For once you've felt the light flow through
You can never go back
To black.

Selected Poems
By Erin Carlyle

Challenger

If my lover wanted to go to space,
I would tell him *no, don't go*. I had a dream

once that my mother was Christa McAuliffe.
I watched her die on TV—my loss

of innocence, my first witness of death.
I felt like my whole body

had blown up in the sky, parts of me
falling to earth in white cloud.

People cried out: *it was the O-ring,*

*the O-ring, and the Solid Rocket
Booster.* If my lover wanted to go,

I would tell him the white
room is not a womb. You won't be

born again to cold space. You'll burn
either going up or coming back

down. You'll burn out like a dead
star, but we'll see it all in real time.

Just a Village Girl

He tells me he'll eat me
up as we cross over

the bridge. The air here is thick. It clings.
My father never told me

about the wolf in the woods,

or that it might put me in a bag,
and throw me over its shoulder.

In my heart, he never locked one
single window, my father, so when

the wolf asked me for a walk, I left
everything behind, and when he said

dark, strange things, I thought
he was just a stupid wolf,

but then the moon got full,
and I realized I left without shoes.

Then the wolf got inside
my belly—bare feet first,

and I had to choose—digest
him or birth him back out.

Joint and Several
By Adam Slavny

Noah's coffee tasted sour, metallic, the flavour of gunmetal. The café was one of those slow haggard places where truckers fill up on plates of greased and gleaming food. Slumped by the side of a road, it was surrounded by scrubby fields and seemed to yawn as the wind passed. A few lone figures sat on plastic chairs, a backlit menu irradiating them with sick white light.

Rosie was nowhere to be seen, and Noah was annoyed at himself for arriving so early--all the more time to stew in the vivid worries that greeted him each morning. He surveyed himself as he waited: a mustard stain nagged at his trouser leg and his jacket was stale and tacky, infused with the odour of his bedroom floor.

Rosie appeared, rattling through the door and raising lethargic glances from around the room. She saw Noah and gave a kind-of smile, approached him, bringing a breeze of perfume with her. She smelt of the coast, the meadow--the outdoors. A face lined and brassy, burnished by sun, was a mark of regular holidays perhaps. She wore a green dress that seemed to widen the scope of her shoulders and a necklace of semiprecious stone threaded with leather strips. She had the appearance of an engraving, Noah thought, deep-set and polished. Just what he expected: that she should be lowered gently into middle age while he fell headfirst into it.

"Your regular?" she asked, looking around doubtfully.

He shrugged. Rosie sat down and the silence between them grew, metastasised.

"How's Louie?" Noah asked eventually.

"He's ok. We're fourteen years next month. How's Beth?"

"You'd have to ask her."

Rosie nodded and said nothing, filling in the gaps for herself. Another of Noah's grim predictions come to pass. She no doubt thought they were self-fulfilling, though she didn't say that. What she did say: "You didn't answer my calls. I even wrote letters. After the trial. Actual, physical letters. You didn't reply to them either. And now suddenly you want a chinwag over coffee?"

He said nothing.

"I assume you want to talk about Herb?"

Noah gripped the table. Absently, his fingers worried something congealed and grainy clinging to its underside. It came off in his hands and he cast it away in disgust.

*   *   *

On a chill autumn afternoon, Rosie followed Herb and Noah through a drooping forest, leaves mulchy underfoot, raindrops plinking through the high lattice branches of the oaks. They were long past anything resembling a path and Rosie was already tired, traversing the forest floor like a true urbanite, threading awkwardly through shrubs, stepping warily over nettles.

She carried a shotgun, barrel nosing through the vegetation as if trying to pick up a scent. It was difficult to focus on the hunt with her own sarcasm still ringing in her ears: "You want me to do *what*, Herb? Killing sentient creatures—oooh, fun!" But despite her initial reluctance, some morbid inner consistency demanded that if she was prepared to carve a dead bird on a plate, she should be prepared to shoot a live one out of the sky.

Plus, hunting was Herb's passion, and he wanted desperately to share it with her and Noah. She suspected it was his way of bringing the three of them together, or at least bringing her and Noah together. At some point Herb would probably wander off and leave the two of them in a clearing framed by sage old oaks, hoping they would fall into each other's arms. The proposition was not entirely unwelcome, she had to admit, though she felt a pang of guilt at the thought of letting Louie down. Sturdy, gracious Louie, who expressed his feelings for her with such matter-of-fact vulnerability that she felt protective towards him, if not loving.

She wondered how Noah felt about Herb's clumsy matchmaking attempts, or about her for that matter. He had spent more time gleaning hunting tips from Herb than talking to her, and she couldn't tell if he was trying to impress her with his prowess or was merely seduced by the challenge of mastering a new skill.

He and Herb now dissected Noah's last attempt in detail. "I moved slowly, like you said," Noah insisted.

Herb dipped his head in agreement. "You did."

"I flushed it out, planted my feet, led my shot. I did everything right. So why didn't I hit it?"

"It was great technique," Herb encouraged. "It was. I'm impressed, kill or no kill."

Rosie gave a grimace of distaste. Noah mumbled something inaudible at the trees, which seemed to whisper behind his back.

*　　*　　*

Sixteen years later, Rosie and Noah sat facing each other sipping their coffee. Noah listened to Rosie talk about Louie, about their life together, forcing out questions. It was hard for him to hear, but anything was better than telling her how he and Beth fell apart and living it again in the retelling. He didn't want to compare marriages--him and Beth, her and Louie--placing them side by side so they could see how his withered on the vine while hers kept reaching for the sun.

Another reason for his questions was the desire for a closure that had long eluded him. He hoped if he learnt enough about her life, it would somehow become real for him, pushing from his mind thoughts of what might have been, dispelling all those ghost futures that haunted him daily. So he pressed on: "And you and Louie were going to try for kids, right?"

She pursed her lips over her coffee and blew perfectly. "We decided against it."

"Thought you always wanted kids?"

"That's not how things turned out." She said it nonchalantly, as if she was not a plant uprooted but a dandelion seed riding the wind. There was the Rosie he remembered, the unruliness, the blasé strength.

A familiar buzzing feeling overcame him, leaving him breathless and dizzy. *Breathe in. And out.* He could feel pressure building in his chest, palms clammy with sweat. A bad time for a panic attack. The café seemed to encircle him, to close in. He was sure the empty chairs were inching closer even though they were bolted to the floor. Piles of white plates, streaked with yellow and brown like soiled halos, teetered on nearby tables. He watched them, hypnotised, wondering which way they would fall.

*   *   *

The oak trees gave way to brushland that hummed with crickets and tall grass prickling the horizon. Herb stared intently at the shrubs, attuned, it seemed, to the passage of unseen creatures. Noah crept along behind him, deep in concentration. Rosie raised her head and closed her eyes against the sky's grey light.

When she opened them again, Noah was quivering with anticipation. A question rose in her but was chased back down when Noah raised his gun. He gave Rosie a brief glance: *get ready.* Then he rustled at the undergrowth and a startled grouse gave a squeal of alarm and flapped into the air.

Rosie found herself tracking its terrified flight with the barrel of her gun. Her brain performed the calculations for her, her muscles moved of their own accord. A beat of preternatural silence, and then the air thunder-clapped twice. Noah had also taken a shot, she realised, though the shots were so close together that they appeared to form a single blast.

When they lowered their guns, Herb had disappeared. Rosie peered at the long grass, a numbness spreading through her limbs. A musty, burning smell rose from the muzzle of her shotgun. She listened, but there was no sound except for the beating of the grouse's wings as it raced towards the open-armed horizon.

"Where's Herb?" Rosie managed, raising a quizzical look from Noah. She started tracking through the brush. The air seemed to shake in the aftershock of their gunfire.

"Herb!" Noah called distractedly, still frustrated at missing his shot.

Then she spotted Herb's boot amongst the willowing grass, its toe pointing upwards. It didn't kick or writhe or even twitch--it was perfectly still. Before she registered what had happened, before she noticed the great blade that had just severed her future from her past, she could not help staring at that motionless boot. It had barely a smear of mud on it. His hunting trousers were also clean and freshly ironed. She took a few steps closer and looked at his face: the high brow, the loose falling hair, the wind-glossed skin. Everything was pristine, except for the little bullet wound beneath the left eye, and for the briefest moment she felt as though she might reach down and simply thumb it away.

*   *   *

In the café, when Rosie had finished updating Noah about Louie, filling him in on all the missing years, she looked at him patiently. For a while he shifted around as if to evade the silence, but eventually he relented: "Beth and I divorced two years ago. Relationship died... oh, at least five years before that. The end was long and drawn-out. No clear time of death."

"I was wondering whether you'd tell me. I heard it through the grapevine, of course."

"It wasn't her fault," he said simply. He didn't elaborate. Didn't say that Beth, too, failed to dodge a bullet, arriving in his life so soon after Herb's death when things had cooled between him and Rosie. That Beth had a mind to salvage him like a piece of wreckage, but found him sunk too deep, embedded too firmly in the ocean floor.

The café had emptied. Outside on the forecourt embittered pigeons fought over scraps. From the bar a waiter watched them idly.

Rosie gave a slow, confessional sigh. "It wasn't easy loosing you as well, so suddenly," she said.

Noah bowed his head, accepted what was coming.

"You just disappeared. I heard you weren't even leaving the house."

"You knew about that?"

"I spoke to Beth on the phone once."

He wondered what that conversation must have been like for Beth, for Rosie, then retreated from both thoughts.

"Does it matter, Noah?" Rosie asked. "Still?"

No reply. He wanted to say it didn't, to let it go. After all, he was the one who invited her here after his countless days indoors, inside a self-made cocoon so tucked and tight it was starting to suffocate him. He had hoped he was finally ready to break free of it, but now she had posed the question directly he was compelled to give her the answer he knew to be true, to rehearse the argument they'd had in the wake of the trial.

"Of course it matters" he said. His trench now dug, he looked at her almost bashfully.

Rosie drew herself up a little. "Neither of us was paying attention to where Herb was standing. We both pulled the trigger without thinking. We did the same thing, Noah."

"We did not do the *same thing*," he hissed, a smear of disgust in his voice. "Only one shot killed him."

She shook her head. "Who cares whose it was? Blind luck, that's all. Let's leave it at that. I know you never believed me, but why didn't you believe the judge in Herb's case? Joint liability, remember? You and me."

Noah chuckled humourlessly. "That's not how I remember it. I think you heard what you wanted to hear. She said *several* liability, not joint. Legally, that means we're responsible for what we did, separately."

"So you're a legal expert now? Then why did we have to pay half and half for the funeral expenses? The damages?"

"Because they couldn't tell whose shot it was," he insisted, feeling old resentments bite the back of his throat like bile. It wasn't that he begrudged paying his half--he knew how it would have looked if Herb's family didn't get a penny just because they couldn't prove which piece of metal killed him. Poor souls fallen between the cracks of legal technicality. Still. The judge's solution neatly sidestepped the question that really mattered: what was the true history of that nugget of lead? Noah pictured it, drawn from the ground, plucked from its ore, fashioned into shot, packed into a cartridge, loaded, triggered, and fired. Its journey from mine to muzzle unknown to them but precise in every detail, its immense weight carried in the chamber of just one gun.

*   *   *

"You could have killed someone!" Rosie's voice rose above the banshee wail of the traffic. The air shimmered as the cars passed, an occasional horn fading into the distance. She had pulled over and lowered her window to yell at the driver of a sportscar who had slowed to a crawl to listen to her tirade with bemused gratification, his vehicle glinting brashly in the sun.

"Some of us can handle our cars," he said, gesturing to Rosie's, which had crookedly mounted the curb where she had pulled over in a fluster. That was all the explanation he gave for overtaking her so suddenly, squeezing through the gap between her car and the one in front with a rush of acceleration. He grinned triumphantly and screeched off.

Images flooded her mind as she watched him drive away. His car losing purchase, spinning out of control and slamming into oncoming traffic, crumpling like tin foil. Smugness whipped from his startled face--she felt the guilty pleasure of it in her blood. Skin hanging from jagged glass. Not his but that of the driver--no, the passenger--of the oncoming car. A daughter being driven home from school, her last conversation with her mother cruelly cut short, launched from the backseat into a windscreen that shatters in a thousand cuts. Her mother, wavering, barely conscious next to her. *His* realisation of what he has done, of the coiled spring he chose to ignore…

Rosie caught sight of her face, sallow and bug-eyed in the rear-view mirror. She felt a sudden desire to strike herself, to knock the images from her mind. Herb had died a year ago and since then she was seeing violence everywhere. In every cracked pavement, waiting to ensnare the wheel of a child's bike; in every open-jawed doorway, waiting to snap off a careless finger; in every plane that flew overhead, waiting to scream and spiral out of the sky.

Risk isn't real, it's hypothetical, Noah had told her after the trial, the last time they spoke, the last time, she felt, that they would ever speak. *Risk is hypothetical. All that matters is what happens.* She leant her head on the steering wheel and sobbed.

*   *   *

The coffee was down to the dregs, the mugs sitting neglected on the table while outside the afternoon was quickly surrendering its light. Perhaps it was the gloom, but Noah thought something in Rosie's expression had changed, that it had softened, or at least eroded.

"We were both careless," she was saying, but her voice was more searching than assertive, her lips quivering slightly. Between words she drew long, ragged, sword-swallowing breaths.

A final push: "You can put anything down to luck if you want, Rosie. It was luck we decided to go hunting on the day we did, that we took that particular route, that we spotted that bird."

Rosie put her head in her hands, pulling her hair taut against her scalp. Noah thought of Beth, her tolerance for him long spent, how he had hounded her about this too.

"I thought we might share this, Noah," Rosie said with a look of grim resignation. "It might have been a lighter load shared between the two of us. Did you ever consider that?"

Seeing her so upset, seeing pain renewed in that bright and brimming face, Noah wondered why he was pushing her so hard.

For the first time in years, he had a memory from before Herb's death: he and Rosie, curled on a sofa, making fun of Herb and his archaic proclivity for hunting. Laughing, bonding over it.

He shifted awkwardly around the table and took Rosie in his arms. For a moment they settled against each other, two bodies in equipoise.

He came back to himself and let her go. A dizziness passed through him, the walls throbbing and pressing, panic whispering its usual threats in his ear. "We'll do this again," he said without conviction. "I'll call." He stuttered a goodbye and slipped quickly through the café door.

*   *   *

When he got to his apartment, Noah turned off the lights to conceal the mess, washed, poured himself a drink, and collapsed into bed. He lay there listening to the pulse of his blood, the drumroll of his heart. After a few sleepless hours, he kicked the covers aside and rolled out of bed. He rifled through some drawers and plucked a case report from a pile of old papers. Herb's appeal: yellow, dog-eared, in some sense still pending.

For years he had thought the judge imposed several liability on them, but Rosie had insisted it was joint. He rubbed his temples as if trying to fasten the legal terminology in his mind. Re-reading the document now, he realised their liability was joint *and* several.

That meant, he gathered, that either of them could be sued by Herb's family and he and Rosie were left to apportion liability in further proceedings, to "fight it out between yourselves" as the judge had translated it in lay terms. Prophetic of her Ladyship, since that's all they had been doing since.

Noah read the case repeatedly until the morning crept up and his room was illuminated in pale, wintry light. Finally he slept and the document slipped from his hand, the logic of its long, laborious judgment scattered across the floor.

He dreamt he was back in the café with Rosie, dimly aware of an unseen threat lurking in the fuzzy space beyond his vision. Herb walked in, tufts of grass tangled up in his hair, the barrel of his gun scraping the floor. Blood glistened around the wound in his upper cheek, a third, weeping eye. Rosie had her back to Herb, oblivious. Noah stared, transfixed, into the muzzle of Herb's gun, but still couldn't tell at whom it was aimed.

Contributors:

Cover Artist:

Hannah Vitiello is a writer and artist from St. Louis, Missouri, with a BA in English from Webster University and an MA in Science Writing from Johns Hopkins University. Her short stories and poetry have been published in *The Green Fuse* and *Sad Girls Club Lit*, and this photograph is her debut as a published photographer. Her photo, "Jellyfish," was taken at a local aquarium under the shifting rainbows of light coloring a tank of translucent jellyfish.

Erin Carlyle is a poet living in Atlanta, Georgia. Her poetry often explores the connections between poverty, place, and girlhood, and can be found in journals such as *Tupelo Quarterly, Ruminate*, and *Prairie Schooner*. Her debut full-length collection, *Magnolia Canopy Otherworld*, is out now on Driftwood Press. She is currently pursuing her PhD in Creative Writing at Georgia State University.

Maria Crimi has lived in New Jersey for most of her life. She has been writing actively for the better part of twenty-five years and has been published in editions of the *Paterson Literary Review* and *Exit 13 Magazine*. She works, writes and hikes in Northwest New Jersey.

Natalie Eckl, originally from Rochester, NY, now lives in Washington, DC where she has recently completed her undergraduate degree in English and creative writing at George Washington University. Her poetry can be found or is forthcoming in *Black Fox Literary Magazine, Five on the Fifth,* and *Tiny Seed Literary Press*.

Samantha Ellis is a young writer from the St. Louis, Missouri area. She has a penchant for writing dreamy narratives that are full of words and phrases that make her feel like her bones have turned to jelly. Some of her work has previously been published in the literary magazines *Currents* and *The Pointed Circle*.

Lily Emerick is a writer and organic farmer located in the Willamette Valley. She holds a Bachelor of Architecture and a BA in Spanish from the University of Oregon. She has most recently been published in *K'in, Call Me Brackets*, and *The Broken City*.

James Engelhardt's poems have appeared in the *North American Review, Hawk and Handsaw, ACM: Another Chicago Magazine, Terrain.org, Painted Bride Quarterly, Fourth River* and many others. His ecopoetry manifesto is "The Language Habitat," and his book, *Bone Willow*, is available from Boreal Books, an imprint of Red Hen Press. He lives in the South Carolina Upstate, does freelance editing, and is a lecturer in the English Department at Furman University.

Benjamin Faro is a green-thumbed writer and educator living in Asunción, Paraguay, on stolen Guaraní lands. He is currently pursuing his MFA at Queens University of Charlotte, and his most recent work appears or is forthcoming in *EcoTheo, Portland Review, Atlanta Review,* and *Sinking City*.

Catheryne Gagnon lives in Montréal/Tio'tia:ke and works in communications in the humanitarian field. Her poetry has been published in *Quail Bell Magazine*. When not writing, she can be found tending to her plants, searching for the best window seat at a café or looking for fireflies in dark woods.

Vanessa Garcia is a multidisciplinary artist working as a screenwriter, novelist, playwright, and journalist. She has written for *Sesame Street, Caillou,* and is a consultant on *Dora the Explorer*. Her plays have been produced in Edinburgh, Miami, Amsterdam, Los Angeles, New York, and other cities around the world. These include the immersive hit, *Amparo* ("Miami's Hottest Ticket," according to People en Español) and her autobiographical radio play, *Ich Bin Ein Berliner* about the fall of the Berlin Wall and Cuba (April 2021). Her novel, *White Light*, was published in 2015, to critical acclaim. Named one of the Best Books of 2015 by NPR, it also won an International Latino Book Award. As a journalist and essayist, her pieces have appeared in *The LA Times, The Miami Herald, The Guardian, The Washington Post, ESPN,* and *The Boston Globe* among numerous other publications. She holds a PhD from the University of California Irvine in English. She is also the co-founder of the production company, Abre Camino Collective. www.vanessagarcia.org

D. Walsh Gilbert is the author of *Ransom* and forthcoming in 2022, *imagine the small bones* (Grayson Books). A Pushcart nominee, she was named winner of The Ekphrastic Review's 2021 "Bird Watching" contest. Her work has recently appeared in *Gleam, The Lumiere Review,* and the anthology, *Waking Up to the Earth: Connecticut Poets in a Time of Global Climate Crisis,* and will be included in *The Poetry Bus*'s 10th Anniversary issue. She serves on the board of the non-profit, Riverwood Poetry Series, and as co-editor of *Connecticut River Review.*

Shreeya Goyal (she/her) is a writer living in California where she attends high school. She has been previously published in the *Aurora Journal* and won the Scholastic Silver Key for her short story, and has plans to pursue English and Social Psychology in her further education. When she is not writing or doing homework, she can be seen preparing for Science Olympiad or Model UN conferences and competitions, or having long-winded conversations about what she reads with her friends.

A.J. Granger is a graduate and former Centennial Scholar of James Madison University with a BA in Media Arts and Design. An avid storyteller and creative, he often dabbles with photography, acting, film editing, and graphic design, while obsessing over shadows and the nuance of perception. Presently, he lives in Hampton Roads, where he is vigorously at work on his first collection of poems. When he is not writing or holding a microscope to his own shadow, he is likely watching the latest Marvel project, singing around the house, and/or drinking a can of Dr Pepper.

Elizabeth Harrison is from St. Andrews West, Ontario. Her poems have been published in *Open Minds Quarterly, The Northern Appeal*, and *untethered magazine*, and are forthcoming in *NōD*. She lives and works in Mississauga, Ontario.

Claire Jussel is a poet, writer, and artist from Boise, Idaho. Her work has appeared in *West Trade Review* and *CP Quarterly*, and she serves as an associate poetry editor at *West Trade Review*. She studied English and history at St. Olaf College and currently resides in Minnesota where she is a bookseller at Wild Rumpus Books in Minneapolis.

Heather Lang-Cassera is Clark County, Nevada, Poet Laureate Emeritus (2019-2021). She is a founder, publisher, and editor of Tolsun Books and is the World Literature Editor and a literary critic for *The Literary Review*. Heather serves Nevada State College as a Lecturer teaching Creative Writing, Professional Editing and Publishing, and more, where she is also a Faculty Advisor for the creative writing club, Blue Sage Writer's Guild, and the literary magazine, 300 Days of Sun. Heather's poetry has been etched into a downtown sidewalk by the City of Las Vegas, and her poems and fiction have been published in *Las Vegas Writes, Lumina, The Normal School, North American Review, Paper Darts, Raleigh Review, South Dakota Review*, and elsewhere. In September of 2021, Unsolicited Press published Heather's full-length poetry collection, *Gathering Broken Light*, the writing of which was supported, in part, by a Nevada Arts Council grant. www.heatherlang.cassera.net

Camille Lebel lives on a small hobby farm outside Memphis, TN where she dabbles in horse whispering and training livestock guardian dogs. Mother to seven, she largely writes in the school pickup line as a way to process special-needs parenting, adoption, religious trauma, and more. She's published or forthcoming in *Inkwell, Sparks of Calliope, Rogue Agent, Literary Mama*, and *Sledgehammer Lit.* You can find her on Instagram @clebelwords

Abigail Leigh is a 27-year-old harpist and poet from Oregon. She is a graduate from Liberty University with a degree in English and Religion. Her pen draws inspiration from life's dichotomies: the belief that light and darkness, growth and decay, joy and sorrow—travel in tandem. She is committed to authentically unveiling truth. Some of her poems have been published in the 16th issue of *Darling Magazine*, as well as on their blog. Find more of her work on Instagram: @thelefthanded.poet

Joshua McKinney's most recent book of poetry is *Small Sillion* (Parlor Press, 2019). His work has appeared in such journals as *Boulevard, Denver Quarterly, Kenyon Review, New American Writing*, and many others. He is the recipient of The Dorothy Brunsman Poetry Prize, The Dickinson Prize, The Pavement Saw Chapbook Prize, and a Gertrude Stein Award for Innovative Writing. He teaches literature and creative writing at California State University, Sacramento. An amateur lichenologist, he is a member of the California Lichen Society.

Alison Mehrman is a communications professional and aspiring writer. She earned her MFA in writing at Lindenwood University where she served as an editorial assistant for *The Lindenwood Review*. She also holds an MS in public relations from Boston University. An ardent storyteller, her feature stories have appeared online and in print for numerous clients, and she is now exploring fiction writing and poetry. Mehrman believes the best writing does more than entertain; it has the power to effect social change. A Massachusetts native, she now lives in Maryland with her family and golden retriever.

Karen McAferty Morris, living in two beautiful places, north Alabama and the Florida panhandle, writes about nature and social issues. Her poetry has been recognized for its "appeal to the senses, the intellect, and the imagination." Her chapbook *Elemental* was published in 2018, followed by *Confluence* in 2020, with

Significance due for publication in 2022, all national prize winners. She is a fan of Billy Collins, Mary Oliver, and Gary Young.

Stephen Page, when he is not writing, reading, spending time with his spouse, communing with nature, or walking his dog, he is making noise with his electric bass. He loves accidentally on purpose losing his cell phone and dog-earing pages in books. He is part Apache, part Shawnee, part Mexican, part English, part Scottish, and part Irish. He graduated from Columbia U (magna cum laude & writing honors) and Bennington College. He has four books of poems, dozens of short stories, countless poems, essays, and literary criticisms published. He is the recipient of The Jess Cloud Memorial Prize for Poetry, a Writer-in-Residence from the Montana Artists Refuge, a Full Fellowship from the Vermont Studio Center, an Imagination Grant from Cleveland State University, a First Place Prize in Poetry from Bravura Magazine, and an Arvon Foundation Ltd. Grant. Twitter: @SmpageSteve

Kim Rose's love of language and literature was sparked during her childhood schooling in the UK. Nowadays, she enjoys a Sunshine State of mind in Gainesville, Florida. A professional strategic/business communicator and consultant, she writes in her spare time and sometimes sings with local rock bands (but mostly in the car on road trips). Her poems have appeared in the *Bacopa Literary Review, Burrow Press, Pittsburgh Poetry Journal* and *Black Fox Literary Magazine*. She's honored to again be featured in BFLM. Follow her on Twitter @kimjayrose.

Claire Scott is an award-winning poet who has received multiple Pushcart Prize nominations. Her work has appeared in the *Atlanta Review, Bellevue Literary Review, New Ohio Review, Enizagam* and *The Healing Muse* among others. Claire is the author of *Waiting to be Called* and *Until I Couldn't*. She is the co-author of *Unfolding in Light: A Sisters' Journey in Photography and Poetry*.

Adam Slavny is an Associate Professor at the University of Warwick and his first academic book is forthcoming with Oxford University Press. His stories are published in *Litro, Storgy, The Welkin* and others, and he has been nominated for a *Best of the Net Anthology*.

Nina Smilow is a recent graduate of Sarah Lawrence's MFA. She writes in all genres about everything. Her work can be seen in *Porridge Magazine* and upcoming in *Literary Mama*.

Joanna Theiss (she/her) is a lawyer turned writer living in Washington, DC. Her publication credits include articles in academic journals and popular magazines. Her short fiction can be found in the pages of *Barren Magazine* and *Bending Genres*, and her website (www.joannatheiss.com) features book reviews and interesting collages. Twitter/Instagram: @joannavtheiss

Marian Willmott is an artist and writer living in Vermont, enjoying both the solitude of the mountains and a vital artistic community. Her work has been published in *Calyx, Salamander, the Denver Quarterly, The Worchester Review, The Louisville Review, Birmingham Arts Journal, and The Comstock Review*, among other journals and in an anthology, *Unbearable Uncertainty. Turnings*, a poetry chapbook, was published by Pudding House Publications in December 2007. *Still Life, Requiem and an Egg*, a poetry chapbook, was published by Prolific Press in 2018. The poem, "In Velvet" was nominated for a Pushcart Prize by the *Worchester Review* in 2014.

Lilian Caylee Wang grew up as a third-culture kid, living in China, Canada, and finally, the states. She won a writing contest as a five-year-old in Tennessee. Since then, her work has been published in the *New York Times, McSweeney's, The Huffington Post, Whetstone Magazine, sPARKLE & bLINK, Solstice Literary Magazine, Five Points Literary, Honey Literary*, and more. She works as a product designer and lives in LA with her partner and her puppy.

Alexander Lazarus Wolff is a student at the College of William & Mary. His work has been published or is forthcoming in *The Best American Poetry* website, *The Citron Review, South Florida Poetry Journal, Main Street Rag, Serotonin,* and elsewhere. You can find him on Facebook at https://www.facebook.com/wolffalex108/ and on Instagram @wolffalex108

Meg Zukin is a writer based in San Francisco. She is currently an MFA candidate at San Francisco State University and works as an editor at *CalMatters*. Her background is in journalism and her work appears in *Variety*, where she worked for nearly three years. She also has upcoming work that will be published in *Flash Fiction Magazine*.

Thank you for reading! Stay in touch:

www.blackfoxlitmag.com
Website

www.facebook.com/blackfoxlit
Facebook

@blackfoxlit
Twitter & Instagram

www.blackfoxlitmag.com/contact/
Newsletter

Check out some of our previous issues:

Resources for Writers from BFLM Editor Racquel Henry's Writer's Atelier:

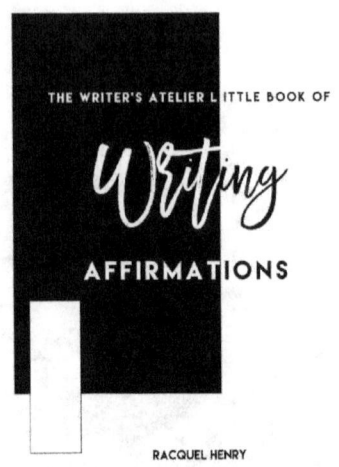

The Writer's Atelier Little Book of Writing Affirmations

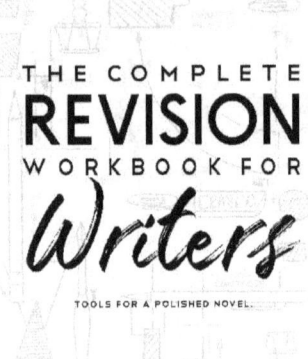

The Complete Revision Workbook for Writers